973.049 Fil
The Filipinos /

34028065138696
PW $34.95 ocm81145400

3 4028 06513 8696
HARRIS COUNTY PUBLIC LIBRARY

JUL 1 1 2007

WITHDRAWN

COMING TO AMERICA

The Filipinos

Other books in the Coming to America series:

COMING TO AMERICA

The Filipinos

Michelle E. Houle, Book Editor

GREENHAVEN PRESS

An imprint of Thomson Gale, a part of The Thomson Corporation

Detroit • New York • San Francisco • New Haven, Conn. • Waterville, Maine • London

Christine Nasso, *Publisher*
Elizabeth Des Chenes, *Managing Editor*

© 2007 Thomson Gale, a part of The Thomson Corporation.

Thomson and Star logo are trademarks and Gale and Greenhaven Press are registered trademarks used herein under license.

For more information, contact:
Greenhaven Press
27500 Drake Rd.
Farmington Hills, MI 48331-3535
Or you can visit our Internet site at http://www.gale.com

ALL RIGHTS RESERVED
No part of this work covered by the copyright hereon may be reproduced or used in any form or by any means—graphic, electronic, or mechanical, including photocopying, record-ing, taping, Web distribution, or information storage retrieval systems—without the written permission of the publisher.

Articles in Greenhaven Press anthologies are often edited for length to meet page require-ments. In addition, original titles of these works are changed to clearly present the main thesis and to explicitly indicate the author's opinion. Every effort is made to ensure that Greenhaven Press accurately reflects the original intent of the authors. Every effort has been made to trace the owners of copyrighted material.

Cover photograph reproduced by permission of Sandy Felsenthal/CORBIS.

ISBN-13: 978-0-7377-3499-7
ISBN-10: 0-7377-3499-X

Library of Congress Control Number: 2006938248

Printed in the United States of America
10 9 8 7 6 5 4 3 2 1

Contents

Chapter 2: The Second Wave of Filipino Immigration

Chapter 4: Accomplished Filipino Americans

Foreword

In her popular novels, such as *The Joy Luck Club* and *The Bonesetter's Daughter*, Chinese American author Amy Tan explores the complicated cultural and social differences between Chinese-born mothers and their American-born daughters. For example, the mothers eat foods and hold religious beliefs that their daughters either abhor or abstain from, while the daughters pursue educational and career opportunities that were not available to the previous generation. Generation gaps occur in almost all families, but as Tan's writings show, such differences are even more pronounced when parents grow up in a different country. When immigrants come to the United States, their initial goal is often to start a new life that is an improvement from the life they experienced in their homeland. However, while these newcomers may intend to fully adapt to American culture, they inevitably bring native customs with them. Immigrants have helped make America broader culturally by introducing new religions, languages, foods, and different ways of looking at the world. Their children and subsequent generations, however, often seek to cast aside these traditions and instead more fully absorb mainstream American mores.

As Tan's writings suggest, the dissimilarities between immigrants and their children are manifested in several ways. Adults who come to the United States and do not learn English turn to their children, educated in the American school system, to serve as interpreters and translators. Children, seeing what their American-born schoolmates eat, reject the foods of their native land. Religion is another area where the generation gap is particularly pronounced. For example, the liturgy of Syrian Christian services had to be translated into English when most young Syrian Americans no longer knew how to speak Syriac. Numerous Jews, freed from the European ghettos they had lived in, wished to assimilate more fully into the surrounding culture and began to loosen the traditional dietary and ritual requirements under which they had grown up. Reformed Judaism, which began in Germany, thus found a strong foothold among young Jews born in America.

However, no generational experiences have been as significant as that between immigrant mothers and their daughters. Living in the United States has afforded girls and young women opportunities they likely would not have had in their homelands. The daughters of immigrants, in some cases, live entirely different lives than their mothers did in their native nations. Where an Arab mother may have only received a limited education, her American-raised daughter enjoys a full course of American public schooling, often continuing on to college and careers. A woman raised in India might have been placed in an arranged marriage, while her daughter will have the opportunity to date and choose a husband. Admittedly, not all families have been willing to give their daughters all these new freedoms, but these American-born girls are frequently more willing to declare their wishes.

The generation gap is only one aspect of the immigrant experience in the United States. Understanding immigrants' unique and shared experiences and their contributions to American life is an interesting way to study the many people who make up the American citizenry. Greenhaven Press's Coming to America series helps readers learn why more people have moved to the United States than to any other nation. Selections on the lives of immigrants once they have reached America, from their struggles to find employment to their experiences with discrimination and prejudice, help give students insights into stereotypes and cultural mores that continue to this day. Finally, profiles of prominent immigrants help the reader become aware of the many achievements of these people in fields ranging from science to politics to sports.

Each volume in the Coming to America series takes an extensive look into a particular immigrant population. The carefully selected primary and secondary sources provide both historical perspectives and firsthand insights into the immigrant experience. Combined with an in-depth introduction and a comprehensive chronology and bibliography, every book in the series is a valuable addition to the study of American history. With immigrants comprising nearly 12 percent of the U.S. population, and their children and grandchildren constantly adding to the population, the immigrant experience continues to evolve. Coming to America is consequently a beneficial tool for not only understanding America's past but also its future.

Introduction

In the twenty-first century Filipino Americans have become the second largest Asian American group in the United States (after Chinese Americans). According to the 2000 U.S. Census, more than 2.4 million Americans identified their ancestry as full or part Filipino. By 2004 the number had increased to 2.7 million. This population of Americans has made contributions in many fields, including business, medicine, and the arts. They have also attained a high level of economic prosperity: A recent survey by the National Filipino American Council found that the median household income and home values of Filipino Americans surpass the national averages in the United States. For example, the average Filipino household earns at least $25,000 annually, in comparison with the national average of $17,200, and owns a house that is worth at least $80,000—which is substantially higher than the national average of $47,200. Furthermore, Filipino Americans have overcome a history of severe discrimination in each of these achievements.

Some of the first Filipinos to immigrate to the United States in large numbers were the *Alaskeros*, who worked in Alaskan fish canneries, and the *sakadas*, who worked on sugar cane plantations in Hawaii in the early 1900s. These Filipino workers were routinely paid less for doing the same backbreaking work as other laborers. Tensions erupted into violent labor strikes in Hawaii and the first organization of Filipino laborers in the U.S. territories.

On the West Coast the first wave of Filipino immigrants also faced hostility from the natives and wage discrimination. As historian H. Brett Melendy notes, "The 1920s saw dramatic changes as California's Filipino population, mostly single young men, increased by 91 percent. . . . Many of these Filipinos experienced significant racial discrimination." This influx of Filipino laborers into California disturbed native Californians who perceived the new arrivals as an economic and social threat. A study published in 1930 by the State of California Department of Industrial Relations argued that Filipinos threatened economic and social interests of Californians, and this report contributed to the climate of discrimination.

In an excerpt from his well-known semiautobiographical novel *America Is in the Heart: A Personal History*, Carlos Bulosan, who emigrated from the Philippines in the 1930s and experienced the hardships of working in low-paying jobs in Alaska and California, describes the harshness of the early treatment of Filipino immigrants:

> I came to know afterward that in many ways it was a crime to be a Filipino in California. I came to know that the public streets were not free to my people: We were stopped each time these vigilant patrolmen saw us driving a car. We were suspect each time we were seen with a white woman. And perhaps it was this narrowing of our life into an island, into a filthy segment of American society, that had driven Filipinos like Doro [Bulosan's companion on the way to Lompoc, California] inward, hating everyone and despising all positive urgencies toward freedom.

As Bulosan illustrates, some white leaders, who opposed the rights of Filipinos to date or marry white women for fear of compromising "racial purity," enacted antimiscegenation laws in many states that banned Filipinos from marrying white women. However, many of these laws were later declared unconstitutional.

Filipino immigrants also faced discrimination in the form of citizenship rights. Although the Philippines had become a possession of the United States in 1898, following the Spanish-American War, Filipinos did not automatically become American citizens. In 1917 an immigration law was passed that stipulated that even though most Filipinos could not become American citizens, they were nationals of the United States rather than aliens and were free to enter the United States from the Philippines. However, in 1935, with growing anti-Filipino sentiment, President Theodore Roosevelt approved the Tydings-McDuffie Act, which reclassified all Filipinos living in the United States as aliens and set the annual quota for Filipino immigrants at fifty. As a result, Filipinos no longer had the right to work legally in the United States. Furthermore, in 1935 Congress also passed the Filipino Repatriation Act, under which the United States offered Filipinos free passage back to the Philippines in an effort to encourage them to leave (this act was finally declared unconstitutional in 1940, after approximately 2,190 Filipinos had returned to the Philippines). Finally, in 1946 Congress voted to allow foreign-born Filipino residents in the United States who had entered the country before March 24, 1934, to become eligible for U.S. citizenship.

Although they have overcome a great deal of discrimination, Filipino Americans today continue to fight prejudices and to correct the mistreatment of the past. One major issue is the question of veterans benefits for Filipino Americans who served in the armed forces during World War II. During this war more than two hundred thousand Filipinos fought to defend the United States against the Japanese and were considered heroic in their efforts to stave off the invaders in the battles of Bataan and Corregidor in the Philippines. More than half of these Filipino enlisted men died during these pivotal fights and had been promised the benefits of those serving in the U.S. armed forces. However, in 1946 Congress passed the Recission Act, which stripped them of these veteran's benefits, and various groups have been fighting ever since to reinstate them. More than thirty thousand Filipino veterans of World War II live in the United States today, most of whom are citizens.

Throughout the 1990s several attempts were made to pass legislation that would have granted veterans benefits to these

World War II servicemen. The Filipino Veterans Equity Act failed in 1995 and again in 1997. On August 3, 2006, Christopher Punongbayan, a lawyer for Filipinos for Affirmative Action, addressed the problem at a community briefing held by the Congressional Asian Pacific American Caucus (CAPAC) in Cupertino, California:

> When Filipinos fought for the U.S. Armed Forces, they formed a contract with the U.S government that in exchange for their service, the veterans would receive U.S. citizenship and would be allowed the same rights and privileges as all other World War II veterans . . . this is why after 59 years, they are seeking equity from the unjust discrimination. They are the only group of World War II veterans who . . . do not receive disability pension, death pension, educational benefits, home buying assistance. and many other privileges that are attached to veterans' status.

As of 2006 there are two acts before Congress that address this issue.

Despite the many challenges that Filipinos have faced in immigrating to America, they continue to come to the United States in large numbers and make many contributions to their new country. In 2005, 36,673 Filipinos became American citizens and were the second biggest group to be naturalized that year. The immigrants who have arrived since 1965 have tended to be highly educated and come in search of professional opportunities. Some have also come to attend college or university in America and have ended up settling here.

The new generation of Filipino Americans born in the United States in general has also sought higher educational opportunities and entered business and professions including engineering, medicine, and economics. However, some commentators and historians have noted that as a group, Filipino Americans tend to lack political power and have not been well represented in higher office; in fact, they are sometimes referred to as "the invisible minority" because most have assimilated into American society quickly, arrive already fluent in English, and have achieved a great deal of economic success. In *Coming to America: The Filipinos* the authors explore in further depth some of the struggles Filipino immigrants have faced, as well as their many accomplishments and other experiences in the United States.

CHAPTER 1

COMING TO
AMERICA

The First Wave of Filipino Immigration

The Philippines Become a Colony of the United States

Amy Blitz

On June 12, 1898, Filipinos independence leader Emilio Aguinaldo declared Philippine independence after years of revolts against Spanish colonial rule. Independence for the Philippines, however, was to be delayed for nearly a half century. According to the terms of a treaty signed at the end of the Spanish American War in 1898, the United States assumed control of the Philippines. Although Filipino nationalists had for years fought for independence from Spain, the Philippines were now to be subject to another colonizing empire, the United States.

In this selection Amy Blitz describes the increase in Filipino resistance as the United States began to assume power. She notes the brutality of U.S. military tactics and describes how Filipino soldiers, under the leadership of Aguinaldo, used guerrilla warfare to resist U.S. forces. The legacy of the colonization and annexation of the Philippines continues to impact the relationship between the Philippines and the United States, she writes.

Amy Blitz is currently director of media development for entrepreneurial studies at Harvard Business School.

American imperialism was hotly contested along partisan lines in the United States [at the beginning of the twentieth century] . . . with Republicans generally supporting it and Democrats generally opposing it. For most of the period from 1899 to 1916, Republicans controlled the presidency and used the authority conferred on the office by congress to appoint Republican governors to manage the Philippines and to establish political, economic, military and social institutions in the

Amy Blitz, "Conquest and Coercion: Early U.S. Colonialism, 1899–1916," in *The Contested State: American Foreign Policy and Regime Change in the Philippines*. Lanham, MD: Rowman & Littlefield, 2000, pp. 31–43. Copyright © 2000 by Rowman & Littlefield Publishers, Inc. All rights reserved. Reproduced by permission.

service of U.S. interests there. When Democrats won the White House under Woodrow Wilson in 1912, however, Filipino nationalists and their allies in the U.S. Congress capitalized on the opportunity for change, pushing through the Jones Act in 1916. They also helped appoint a Democratic governor who would loosen U.S. control of the colonial government in the Philippines and pave the way for eventual self-rule.

Transition to U.S. Colonial Rule

Prior to the U.S. Congressional vote [February 6, 1899] on ratification of the Paris Peace Treaty, which accorded the United States the right to purchase the Philippines from Spain for $20 million, tensions had mounted between Filipino and U.S. forces surrounding Manila. Tensions reached a pitch in January 1899, when Major General Elwell Otis, head of the U.S. operations, moved the Nebraska regiment to an area inside territory claimed by the Filipinos. Though [President William] McKinley had directed the troops to preserve the peace, Otis authorized his troops to use force if necessary for self-defense. On the evening of February 4, 1899, while on a routine patrol, Private William Grayson of Beatrice, Nebraska stumbled upon four drunk, unarmed Filipinos. When he ordered them to halt, the Filipinos mocked him. Grayson repeated the order and again the response was mocking. Grayson fired and one man was felled. Grayson's partner, Orville Miller, shot another while Grayson reloaded and shot a third Filipino. Miller and Grayson then rushed back to camp to inform the other Nebraskans. Within minutes, war exploded along the ten-mile front separating United States and Filipino forces near Manila. "The ball has begun," yelled one Major Wilder Metcalf of Kansas. Two days later, the U.S. Congress narrowly voted to ratify the Paris Treaty, as a war to subdue Filipino nationalists raged. The United States would confidently term the struggle the "Philippine Insurrection," dismissing the insurgents as *ladrones* or bandits. Ultimately, however, the war would serve as a cautionary tale to American expansionists regarding the frailty of a European treaty in the face of nationalist opposition abroad as well as anti-imperialist opposition at home.

Immediately following the Grayson incident, U.S. regiments of volunteers from Kansas, Idaho, California, Montana and Pennsylvania captured bridges, Filipino arsenals and other key strategic sites. In the process, they leveled nipa huts and churches, and slaughtered roughly 3,000 Filipinos in the first day of fighting, while U.S. troops suffered only minor losses, including 59 dead and 300 wounded. U.S military officials issued forecasts that the war could be won quickly, with little loss of American lives. Meanwhile, [Filipino nationalist Emiliano] Aguinaldo, stunned, sent two representatives to offer a truce, the creation of a buffer zone and peace talks. Otis rebuffed these offers and turned instead to the business of war. Although President McKinley had not clearly stated whether the aim of U.S. forces was to control Manila or the entire archipelago, Otis expanded the conquest, ordering troops to seize the port in Iloilo and the nearby Visayan Islands of Cebu and Negros. An alliance was also formed between the U.S. forces and Macabebe soldiers, the long-time military aides to Spain, who acted as scouts and helped carry out the military policies of the war. Still, American military strength totaled just 24,000 men, about a third of the number mobilized by Aguinaldo. To manage military strategy, administration of U.S. policy towards the Philippines now shifted from the State Department to the Department of War, as McKinley issued his "benevolent assimilation" proclamation:

> It should be the earnest wish and paramount aim of the military administration to win the confidence, respect, and affection of the inhabitants of the Philippines by assuring them in every possible way that full measure of individual rights and liberties which is the heritage of free peoples,

and by proving to them that the mission of the United States is one of benevolent assimilation, substituting the mild sway of justice for arbitrary rule.

Philippine Resistance

Unfortunately, such benevolence did not extend to the battlefield. U.S. forces inflicted terrible casualties on Aguinaldo's troops, easily overcoming entrenchments that were "beautifully made and wretchedly defended," [according to historian Brian Linn] as Aguinaldo's choice of conventional rather than guerrilla tactics proved increasingly untenable. Despite heavy losses, however, Aguinaldo continued to control the main island of Luzon and maintained a favorable ratio of about two Filipino soldiers to every one American, as the U.S. forces soon learned that they could win battles but could not hold territory. The first major offensive of the war, launched by Brigadier General Lloyd Wheaton in March, was carried out with efficiency and exacted a heavy toll on the revolutionaries; but it also revealed the breadth and effectiveness of the opposition. Afterwards, Otis was forced to concede that he did not have enough troops to wage war in the interior, nor to occupy territories captured there, and still defend Manila. By the end of March, U.S. troops under the command of Brigadier General Arthur MacArthur captured Malolos, seat of Aguinaldo's government, only to have Aguinaldo relocate the capital to San Fernando in Pampanga province. As one American journalist wrote, Aguinaldo simply "took up the goal-posts and carried them back," whenever U.S. forces advanced. In spite of early U.S. military forecasts of a quick and easy victory, Otis now struggled to proclaim success while simultaneously, and somewhat paradoxically, requesting additional troops. Concerned that he would be replaced should officials back home learn the truth, Otis increasingly exercised the right of press censorship that the War Department had conferred upon him.

Though coverage of the U.S. campaign in the Philippines was initially favorable since the early reporters relied almost exclusively on U.S. military sources, it became more and more negative after the rainy season descended in the Spring, bringing with it a host of tropical diseases. The correspondents now began to hear of illness as well as atrocities of the war from the men at the front; yet the military continued to announce victories known to be fictitious, while issuing false reports on the number of U.S. casualties. Disillusioned, the journalists sought alternative sources of information, particularly from soldiers returning from the "boondocks," from the Tagalog *bundok* or mountains. By early summer, the correspondents complained of "wholly ridiculous estimates" of enemy killed and other misrepresentations of the war, while Otis criticized the press for trying to influence opinion back home and for playing into the hands of the enemy. Otis now ordered censorship of dispatches sent via the trans-Pacific cable that was controlled by the U.S. military and was at the time the only direct line of communication to the United States. With the censors allowing less and less to pass through, the correspondents, led by Robert Collins of Associated Press, drafted a statement in July protesting that Otis was feeding the American public "an ultra-optimistic view that is not shared by the general officers in the field." Though Otis threatened court-martial for "conspiracy against the government," the statement was transmitted to American journals via Hong Kong, and even pro-imperialist papers printed it. McKinley publicly backed Otis but instructed Secretary of War Elihu Root to urge Otis to adopt more liberal press policies. Instead, Otis continued to withhold cable privileges to any reporter who implied, as most American soldiers now believed, that the U.S. forces in the Philippines were inadequate. . . .

War Atrocities

Meanwhile, letters home from soldiers at the front spoke of the brutality of the U.S. troops as well as the much higher levels of U.S. casualties than the government had been reporting, all undermining the credibility of and support for the U.S. operations in the Philippines. When U.S. officials tried to intercept mail, further outcries about freedom of speech were heard, as attention to the subject mounted in the press. By the Spring of 1899, when many of the volunteers were becoming eligible for discharge, the cry to bring home the troops had mushroomed in the Northwest and South, while disaffection spread as well among the troops. Only about 7 percent were expected to reenlist.

As U.S. troops became more and more mired in the war abroad, opposition at home continued to grow. The Anti-Imperialist League now had about 40,000 members nationwide, and opposition spread even among former imperialists. Senator Frye of Maine, for example, publicly said he felt "deceived" by the military's initial claims of easy victory, while General Frederick Funston began to sense from the battlefield no benefit of the war save for "big syndicates and capitalists." Meanwhile, many African-Americans and their supporters linked war atrocities with the growing problem of lynchings and other racial violence in the United States, as former abolitionists linked suppression of Filipino nationalism to the issues for which the Civil War had been fought just a few decades earlier. By October 1899, the League was a national organization with an eye toward the upcoming 1900 elections. Democratic candidate William Jennings Bryan had earlier tried to focus primarily on the free silver issue, but now made opposition to the war in the Philippines a centerpiece of his presidential campaign, rallying labor, African-Americans, and others to the anti-imperialist cause.

October 1899 also brought the fiercest battles of the war, as Otis launched an all-out effort to destroy Aguinaldo's army. On the main island of Luzon, Otis ordered one division to head south from Manila while another, led by General Arthur MacArthur, headed north. American soldiers then took Aguinaldo's newest capital on October 12, forcing the rebels to move once more. Days later, the United States captured that capital, only to have Aguinaldo merely skip away yet again. Though the United States prevailed in most battles, Otis conceded: "Little difficulty attends the act of taking possession of and temporarily holding any section of the country.... but (the U.S. troops) would.... again prey upon the inhabitants, persecuting without mercy those who had manifested any friendly feelings towards the American troops." Thus, American conduct fueled opposition both at home and in the Philippines, a problem that grew when the war took a new turn.

Guerrilla Tactics

In November 1899, forced to concede that a conventional approach could only fail, Aguinaldo ordered his troops to scatter and adopt guerrilla tactics. In part, Aguinaldo was playing for time, hoping, like his U.S. anti-imperialist counterparts, that the 1900 U.S. presidential elections might usher in a new, Democratic administration open to peace and, perhaps, to an independent Philippines. Otherwise, he hoped to simply wear down the Americans through a war of attrition. Leading one of the larger groups, a contingent of 1,200, Aguinaldo fled into the mountains. Waging a guerrilla war had the advantage of keeping the Americans on the run, as Filipino forces easily blended in with the populace, making it difficult for the U.S. forces to distinguish friend from foe, but it had disadvantages as well. The military reversals of the past months had reduced the numbers as well as the appeal of Aguinaldo's campaign; yet now more than ever Aguinaldo's troops were dependent upon the masses of Filipinos for protection and support. At first, Aguinaldo revived the Katipunan as an agency to enforce revolutionary codes and punish collaborators. Soon, however, the Katipunan dispensed with trials for suspected collaborators, declaring it the policy of the revolution to simply "exterminate all traitors." Meanwhile, U.S. forces used increasingly gruesome methods such as the "water cure" to force information from potential informants, who eventually included almost everyone in the countryside. Now Filipinos risked punishment from the Americans for keeping quiet and assassination by the revolutionaries for talking. Given that choice, most apparently found greater safety as well as prospective gains in the revolutionary cause, which remained strong, as ever more U.S. troops were needed to combat it.

At top levels, however, dissent among the revolution's leaders threatened the movement, as it had in the final phases of the uprising against Spain. Now, as then, the ilustrados and other Filipino elites grew concerned that their own social, political and economic interests might be threatened by the spreading rebellion in the countryside. Though Aguinaldo consistently favored the elites in the countryside, allowing them to keep estates confiscated from the Spanish while granting them exclusive political rights, top ilustrados began defecting from the revolutionary movement, particularly after Aguinaldo switched from conventional to guerrilla warfare. . . .

Enforced American "Supremacy"

As early as January 1899, following advice from [Admiral George] Dewey, McKinley had established an official civilian Philippine Commission to study the situation and possibly avert warfare. . . . Arriving in March, one month after the outbreak of hostilities, the Philippine Commission was too late for diplomacy, and Otis argued that the onset of fighting annulled the commission's authority. . . .

On April 4, after just one month of research, the commission published its initial findings, offering the revolutionaries a modicum of political autonomy under U.S. colonial rule, as well as public works projects, a revitalized judicial system, universal education, economic development programs, and other reforms. At the same time, the commission threatened that American "supremacy" would be "enforced" throughout the Philippines, and that those who resisted would "accomplish no end other than their own ruin." The revolutionary leadership publicly rejected the commission's offer, but quietly approached the commission to offer a ceasefire. Though [head of the Philippine Commission Jacob Gould] Schurman urged U.S. officials to explore the peace bid, Otis, as he had at the war's outbreak, rebuffed the Filipino offer. [Commission members Charles] Denby and [Dean] Worcester, and subsequently McKinley, concurred. Hard-line not soft-line strategies now prevailed.

Otis did realize that force alone could not subdue the revolutionaries, however, and he continued the kinds of sanitation, education, and public works projects as well as food distribution programs and judicial reforms first launched a year earlier during the occupation of Manila. . . . He also began organizing town councils comprised of the Filipino elites Aguinaldo had helped promote in the 1898 elections. This was done through limited suffrage, with U.S. officers in charge. At the same time the Philippine Commission continued its work through the long rainy season, the worsening conditions of war, and the increasingly negative dispatches from the correspondents, which led, in turn, debate back home. Though Schurman continued to press for diplomacy, Denby and Worcester argued for an intensification of the military campaign. Concurring with the hard-liners, McKinley ordered additional troops. By the summer of 1899, the U.S. troops numbered 60,000. . . .

At the end of 1900, U.S. troop levels reached 70,000, about three quarters of the entire U.S. Army. By late 1900, several of Aguinaldo's best officers had either surrendered or had been captured and now swore allegiance to the United States. A key goal for U.S. forces was now the capture of Aguinaldo. In February 1901, the opportunity came. That month, a Filipino courier, with a coded letter from Aguinaldo requesting additional troops and describing his location, was captured. Using the information, General Funston, with MacArthur's approval, devised a plan involving eighty Macabebe [a municipality in Pampanga, Philippines] soldiers. On March 24, the Macabcbcs posed as partisans and, together with a group of Americans posing as their prisoners, entered Aguinaldo's secret encampment. Once inside, the Macabebes and Americans easily defeated Aguinaldo's inner network of supporters. They then captured Aguinaldo and brought him to MacArthur's headquarters at the Malacanang palace. There Aguinaldo swore allegiance to the United States and urged his followers to do the same, though he would wear a black bow tie forever after until his death in 1964 as an expression of mourning for his lost republic. The resistance, though seriously weakened, nevertheless continued.

U.S. Military Government Established

In March 1901, a revised version of the Spooner Bill, now an amendment to a military appropriations bill, passed, empowering the President of the United States to continue to administer the Philippines until such time as Congress enacted legislation establishing a permanent colonial government there. A few months later, on July 4, 1901, [President William Howard] Taft, who had actively lobbied from the Philippines and in the United States for such an amendment, became governor of the Philippines, while MacArthur was replaced by Major General Adna R. Chaffee. The new division of authority granted Taft control of civil government in areas that had been pacified and Chaffee control of military government where the war still raged. Two weeks later, on July 18, the United States established the Insular Police Force to create a native organization capable of suppressing revolutionary opposition, as the existing transnational authoritarian alliance with the Macabebes became institutionalized. Under the command of Captain Henry Allen, the force numbered 180 Americans reinforced by carefully recruited Filipinos, notably Macabebes. The Spooner Amendment was not to apply long to McKinley, however. In September, he was shot by presumed anarchist Leon F. Czolgosz. McKinley died eight days later, on September 14, and Theodore Roosevelt, the man who had engineered the conquest of the Philippines, ascended to the presidency.

More severe hard-line policies were now introduced. On November 4, for example, Taft passed the Sedition Law, which imposed either the death sentence or a long prison term on anyone advocating independence, even by peaceful means, while allowing for severe fines and punishment for anyone uttering "seditious words or speech" against the U.S. government. All parties except the Federalistas were also banned. Even worse, on December 25, General Franklin Bell directed his commanders to set up reconcentration zones to closely monitor the comings and goings of the roughly 300,000 inhabitants of the Batangas region. All property outside the zones was confiscated, and the people were herded into the camps. It was a desperate attempt to isolate the insurgents from the general populace, but, with the hostile and unsanitary conditions that quickly resulted in the zones, the policy instead further fueled revolutionary opposition to the United States. It also fueled opposition back home since the main impetus behind the war with Spain had allegedly been to undo Spain's harsh reconcentration policy in Cuba.

The war was to drag on through the early months of 1902, with U.S. tactics becoming increasingly brutal. These tactics were effective in the Philippines, seriously weakening the revolutionary opposition there; but, as word spread to the U.S. public, via newspaper correspondents and letters home from soldiers at the front, domestic U.S. opposition exploded into a political and social crisis much like that experienced generations later over U.S. policy in Indochina. One massacre on the island of Samar in late 1901 had gained particular notoriety. While the U.S press ranked it with the Alamo and Custer's last stand as one of the worst tragedies in American military history, congressional hearings were initiated in January 1902 under the direction of Senator Hoar. Confirming the worst fears of the anti-imperialists, Major Littleton Waller Tazewell Waller revealed orders he had been given by Brigadier General Jacob Smith to kill everyone over the age of ten and to make the island of Samar a "howling wilderness." Smith was the only U.S. soldier to be disciplined for conduct in the Philippine war and, at that, was merely "admonished," yet the outrage expressed in the United States chastened U.S. imperialists. Resistance in the Philippines continued sporadically over the next months, and indeed would continue for the next decade before dying out then reemerging in various forms by the 1920s. Nevertheless, the war was brought to a formal conclusion on July 4, 1902, though 50,000 U.S. soldiers remained to suppress the ongoing, albeit diffused resistance.

War Casualties

In all, 126,000 Americans took part in the war, with a toll of 4,234 dead, 2,818 wounded, thousands succumbing to disease once home, and some $600 million spent on the war effort. For Filipinos, the toll was much greater, with the number of deaths estimated at between 200,000 and 600,000, 90 percent of all carabaos—a critical farm animal—dead, the rice harvest down to one-fourth normal levels, and vast areas of the countryside in ruin. Despite the desperately fought bid for independence, the Filipinos were forced to cede control of their country to a new colonial power.

The Earliest
Filipino Immigrants

Barbara M. Posadas

In this selection Barbara M. Posadas describes the first wave of Filipino immigrants to the United States. Between 1903 and 1935, more than 125,000 Filipino nationals went to work on plantations in Hawaii and fisheries in Alaska. The work of cutting sugar cane was often brutal, and plantation owners exploited their workers through low wages and poor working conditions, Posadas writes. Other Filipino immigrants sought work in the farmlands of California, where they also often encountered economic hardships and discrimination. These first Filipino immigrants who came to the United States and the American territory of Hawaii called themselves pinoys. *Posadas also describes the Filipino students, or* pensionados, *who came to the United States to study at the beginning of the twentieth century.*

Barbara M. Posadas is a professor of history at Northern Illinois University, DeKalb. She also serves as the director of the Filipino American National Historical Society and is a member of the editorial boards of Amerasia *and the* Journal of American Ethnic History.

Immediately after American acquisition of the Philippines from Spain in 1898, Filipinos began arriving in the United States and Hawaii (then an American possession). Typically, Filipinos came either to earn American dollars or to obtain an American education. With varying degrees of success, some combined schooling and work on the mainland. Virtually all originally intended to return to the Philippines, but many temporary sojourners ultimately became lifelong immigrants,

Barbara M. Posadas, "Filipinos in the United States before 1965," in *The Filipino Americans*. Westport, CT: Greenwood Press, 1999, pp. 13–24. Copyright © 1999 by Barbara M. Posadas. All rights reserved. Reproduced by permission of Greenwood Publishing Group, Inc., Westport, CT.

establishing families and communities far from home. The *Pinoys,* as Filipinos living in the United States before World War II called themselves, also came to be known as the "old-timers" decades later, thus distinguishing them from the Filipino immigrants who arrived after 1965.

Earliest Filipino Immigrants

Prior to 1898, an undetermined number of Filipinos, called *indios* during the Spanish colonial period, arrived in the Americas and settled in territory that would ultimately become the United States, as well as in Mexico. Between 1565 and 1815, four years after Mexico won independence from Spain, galleons travelled between Manila and Acapulco, manned by crews that included Philippine natives. Thus, Filipinos participated in voyages of discovery along the Pacific Coast. "Luzon indians" accompanied Pedro de Unamuno when he landed at Morro Bay on the California coast in 1587. Three centuries later, in *Harper's Weekly* in 1883, [author] Lafcadio Hearn wrote of "Malay fishermen—Tagalas from the Philippine Islands" living in the bayous of Louisiana.

Direct continuity between the *indios* on the galleons and the Filipinos in the bayous has never been proven, but the work of [historian] Marina E. Espina indicates that by 1898 a handful of Filipinos and their descendants were well established in the New-Orleans area.

The vast majority of Filipinos who left their homeland before the mid-1930s were set in motion by the integration of the Philippines into the capitalist world market as an agricultural export economy. The process, which began under late eighteenth-century Spanish rule, grew more intense under American sway. As the production of export crops, such as sugar, *abaca*, tobacco, and coffee, on large-scale plantations became increasingly important, both to colonial rulers and to Filipino elites, the growing of rice by small-scale farmers declined, and "tenancy and landlessness" rose [according to historian Miriam Sharma].

Employment in Hawaii

Displaced agricultural workers came first to Hawaii, where the Hawaiian Sugar Planters Association (HSPA) experimented with the importation of Filipino workers as early as 1906. At the turn of the century, Hawaiian sugar growers had depended heavily on Japanese labor. By 1910, a shift to Filipino labor had begun. Growers actively recruited Filipino contract workers, called *sakadas*, out of fear that their continuing access to cheap Japanese labor would be restricted by a government ban on their future entry. By 1915, Filipinos were 19 percent of sugar plantation employees; by 1922, 41 percent; and in 1932, 69.9 percent, by which time, Japanese workers in sugar had declined to 18.8 percent.

Between 1909 and 1934, the HSPA imported 118,556 *sakadas* into Hawaii—103,513 men, 8,952 women, and 6,091 children—large numbers from the Ilocano-speaking provinces of northern Luzon. By 1935, 58,281 had returned to the Philippines. Still, despite poor wages, dreadful working conditions, and continuing agitation for improvement which led to the deportation of labor leader Pablo Manlapit in 1935, those *sakadas* who remained, along with their offspring, established thriving, ethnically based communities throughout Hawaii.

Prior to World War II, Filipinos in Hawaii consistently outnumbered those in the mainland United States, although by 1940, the gap was narrowing. The large number of pre-1935 Hawaii-to-mainland transmigrants indicates the likely possibility that at least a third of the 45,876 Filipinos living in the United States in 1940 had worked first in Hawaii. After they arrived in the mainland, many of these laborers most likely found seasonal jobs in agriculture in the Pacific Coast states and as so-called *alaskeros* [Filipinos who came to work in Alaska] in the canneries of Alaska, as did many others who came directly from the Philippines.

For the price of a ticket across the Pacific, a worker could journey to the United States free of any constraints imposed by immigration legislation. Unlike Chinese and Japanese laborers, already or soon to be excluded by anti-Asian immigration policies, Filipinos—whatever their economic class—might, as U.S. nationals, enter without restriction. Soon, Filipino workers became an attractive labor source for West Coast employers in agriculture, in salmon canning, and in service occupations.

Filipinos on the Mainland

By contrast with Hawaii, the first Filipinos to arrive in the mainland after the turn of the century were students, initially the sons of elite Filipinos. Just as American colonial administrators worked to establish a system of public education in the Philippines during the early decades of the century, so too did they emphasize education for a chosen few in the United States as essential to their aim of binding current and future Filipino leaders to the American colonial administration.

In 1900, before the end of the Philippine-American War, Philippine Commission member Dean C. Worcester suggested that Manila's elite *Club Internacional de Manila* sponsor a competitive examination to select several students for education in the United States. Before the year ended, the first three journeyed across the Pacific aboard a U.S. Army transport ship, en route to their destination, Ann Arbor, Michigan.

Their stories of the "ludicrous situations" and financial straits into which naive Filipinos might blunder in foreign territory were probably among the first youthful accounts to reach their homeland—the three watermelons they ordered at a San Francisco hotel, thinking that each would be an individual's portion—the dime rubber collars they wore to cut their laundry bills—the ill-fitting suit one bought on an installment plan. If such tales both entertained and instructed, the story of their ultimate success, credited to hard work and persistence in an unfamiliar land, seemingly set an example that others might follow.

The *Pensionados*

Established in 1903, the *pensionado* program provided government scholarships to students supposedly chosen by merit from each Philippine province; in actuality, local prominence and connections played a major role in the selection process. In return for each year of education in the United States, *pensionados* were required to work for the government in the Philippines for the same length of time.

The initial and largest group, the 104 young men who departed the Philippines in 1903 spent their first school year (1903–1904) in close proximity, living with families while attending California schools. Perhaps most important to their future success, according to William Alexander Sutherland, who had them in his personal charge, they made a "record . . . of credit to themselves and to their race."

In August 1904, the *pensionados* spent a month at the St. Louis World's Fair where they served three hours per day "as guides to visitors in the different Philippine buildings" [according to a 1905 report by Superintendent Alex. Sutherland]. During the World's Fair, public interest in the Philippines focused particularly on the Philippine Reservation where ethnological villages displayed the seeming barbarism and savageness of the "wild tribes," especially the Igorots' and Negritos' lack of clothing. The *pensionados* counteracted both the impression and the argument. Indeed, the St. Louis World's Fair would be just one occasion when Filipino students found themselves upholding their people and their nation.

Pensionado stories became legend, fueling the migration of larger numbers of Filipino students during the next decades. The individual triumphs they achieved in the service of their homeland upon their return from America marked them, for Filipinos and Americans alike, as the leaders of a nation in the making. Their competence over the years seemed to offer a tangible realization of both the loftiest and the most self-interested goals of U.S. foreign policy on one hand and a concrete proof of the capability of the Filipino people on the other.

Students in the 1920s

By the early 1920s, unlike the period immediately after the turn of the century, far fewer Filipino students enjoyed complete support, their numbers eclipsed by the many more who were self-supporting. Two examples can illustrate the differences between those who enjoyed either family or scholarship support and those who had to support themselves. Fully funded by his wealthy family, Carlos Quirino, later a prominent author, remembered his years at the University of Wisconsin in Madison where he earned a journalism degree "as a series of tennis games rather than classes." In contrast, his contemporary and friend, Agustin Rodolfo, lived "in the Animal Husbandry laboratory . . . [where he kept] his clothes, a Bunsen burner for heating soup and a toaster. At night he slept with a close friend in a bit of forest by the shore of Lake Mendota. When the weather forced them to seek shelter, they retired to the boathouse which they owned in common, or to the canoe kept there" according to historians Barbara M. Posadas and Roland L. Guyotte. Although Rodolfo, like Quirino, ultimately earned his degree and returned to establish a career as an educator in the Philippines, countless others did not achieve their original educational goals and instead became "unintentional immigrants."

In urban locales, Filipinos who hoped to succeed as self-supporting students filled niches in local economies, typically as service workers in restaurants, hotels, and private clubs, and as personal servants. Occasionally, Filipinos found factory work, perhaps the largest number in the Detroit area working for the Ford Motor Company.

During the 1920s and the 1930s, as today, most Filipinos lived on the West Coast. Some came, as they did to the Midwest, to continue their educations; others, to make money. Some travelled, following jobs locally, while others moved in their youth among regions, not quite transient, but never quite permanent. Born in 1896 in La Union province and already nearing forty when he "rode steerage" to the United States, Julio Orille left school after the second grade. Arriving in California in 1934 and moving frequently before World War II, he worked in a county hospital in San Jose; dug a garden, picked strawberries and prunes, washed dishes, and picked "tomatoes, lettuce, squash and other vegetables," all in the Sacramento area; raised "cabbage, cauliflower, broccoli and sprouts" on a farm near Half Moon Bay; picked tomatoes again near San Jose; and worked in a nursery in Redwood City and in a cafeteria in San Francisco. "I didn't write many letters home but I always sent money [Orille recalled]." During these years, [Orille notes that] he also "went to school a lot"—"to improve my English" [according to a note by historian Roberto V. Vallangea].

Anti-Filipino Discrimination

Those who did successfully complete their educations sometimes found their entry into their chosen profession barred by discrimination. Having worked as a janitor while he earned his civil engineering degree, one Filipino proudly displayed his diploma on the wall of his apartment where his children could see it, but continued to work as a janitor.

Pervasive social and economic hostility against Filipinos in California, described in [author] Carlos Bulosan's *America Is in the Heart* (1946), erupted most severely at Watsonville in January 1930. During five days of violence, gunmen firing from a passing car peppered a camp barracks with shots and killed Filipino farmworker Fermin Tobera as he lay in his bunk.

In California, Arizona, Idaho, Nevada, Utah, and Wyoming, as well as in Georgia, Mississippi, Missouri, and South

Dakota, state legislatures passed anti-miscegenation statutes forbidding marriage between "white" and "Mongolian" partners. Recalling California in the 1930s, [Filipino American] Paul Valdez remembered: "They used to pass out leaflets saying that the Japanese were taking the lands from the Americans, the Chinese were taking the businesses, and the Filipinos were taking the women". If a couple lived in a restrictive state, they could circumvent the prohibition by marrying in another state, as did the Filipino father and English immigrant mother of Olympic gold medalist Victoria Manolo Draves. Born in San Francisco in 1924, she was forced to hide her Filipino heritage and use her mother's maiden name, Taylor, when she began competing, because of hostility against Filipinos.

Filipinos in the Military

Filipinos also enlisted in branches of the U.S. military before World War II. By 1901, with the Philippine-American War still under way, over 5,500 Filipinos were serving as Philippine Scouts under American officers in the regular army. In 1904, 1,369 Scouts, on detachment from their regular postings in the Philippines, became a much-applauded part of the Philippine Exhibit at the St. Louis World's Fair.

In 1904, the U.S. Navy began recruitment of Filipinos— just over 300 in that year. Thereafter, Filipino numbers grew steadily, never falling below 3,900 between 1918 and 1933. In 1922, the navy's 5,018 Filipinos constituted 5.7% of the enlisted force. Filipinos became known as "superior servants"—so "superior" that the navy stopped its enlistment of African American messmen in 1919. In 1932, when Filipinos numbered 3,922, only 441 African Americans remained in the service. But Filipinos quickly found that their own race also circumscribed their opportunities for advancement. In 1920, the Bureau of Navigation informed the commanding officer of the Hampton Roads Naval Training Station "that it was 'contrary to the Bureau's policy to rate filipinos in any branches other than the messmen and musicians branches.'" Despite such obvious discrimination, many Filipinos found lifelong careers and undoubtedly enjoyed more security in the navy than did most compatriots who lived in the United States during these years.

Obstacles to Citizenship

Despite their ability as U.S. nationals to migrate freely, those born in the Philippines were not eligible to become citizens of the United States. Naturalization had been "limited to free white persons" in 1790, a policy liberalized prior to the outbreak of World War II only for African Americans—by ratification of the Fourteenth Amendment in 1868—and for African immigrants—by passage of the Naturalization Act of 1870. Thus, although all children born in the United States to Filipino immigrants were U.S. citizens, before World War II, no matter how many years Philippine-born Filipinos had lived in the United States, they were ineligible for naturalization, and, therefore, could not vote, or be absolutely sure of their future status and security.

In the mid-1930s, Filipinos in the United States also faced a more tenuous legal situation. The Tydings-McDuffie Act of 1934 promised the Philippines independence after ten years (a pledge not kept, because of World War II, until 1946), but immediately restricted immigration from the Philippines to a fifty per year quota. After independence, Filipino immigrants, like all other Asians, were to be totally excluded, although a clause (invoked in 1946) permitted Hawaii's sugar planters to recruit labor in the Philippines if they could demonstrate a need. Filipinos already in the United States now knew that they could never visit their homeland, even to see a dying parent, without relinquishing their right to return to the United States. During the Depression, Congress also passed the Repatriation Act of 1935, which allocated federal funds for the transport of Filipinos who would voluntarily return to the Philippines. Fewer than 2,200 Filipinos took the government's offer.

Educational Opportunities for Filipinos in America

Dorothy B. Fujita-Rony

The opportunity for higher education motivated many Filipino nationals to move to the United States in the early twentieth century. As Dorothy B. Fujita-Rony describes in this selection, under American colonial rule, educational opportunities became more accessible to Filipinos than ever before—especially for males. The American government set up public schools at the primary, intermediate, and secondary levels throughout the Philippines. In addition, Fujita-Rony writes, the U.S. government created the pensionado *program, which offered select Filipino males the opportunity to earn a university education in return for service to the government. Education was seen by U.S. government officials as a means to assimilate Filipinos and assist their transition into American life. In this selection Filipinos who came to the United States for educational reasons recall their experiences.*

Dorothy B. Fujita-Rony is an associate professor of the Asian American Studies department and affiliate to the history department at the University of California, Irvine.

Of all the factors that would mark Filipina/os as different from the first generation of other groups who migrated to the American mainland and Hawai'i, the widespread emphasis on university education because of American colonialism in the Philippines would be a crucial distinction. While education was an important value for Asian Americans as a whole, particularly because of its connection to class mobility, it is important to recognize how in the Filipina/o case, educa-

Dorothy B. Fujita-Rony, "Education in the Metropole," in *American Workers, Colonial Power: Philippine Seattle and the Transpacific West, 1919–1941*. Berkeley: University of California Press, 2003, pp. 51–56. Copyright © 2003 by the Regents of the University of California. Reproduced by permission.

tion in the United States was seen as an extension of education in the Philippines. Belen DeGuzman Braganza was one such early pioneer who received a university education in Seattle. She was born in 1913 in Manila, the second oldest of five siblings. Her father was an architect, but he died when Braganza was only seven years old. Braganza's mother supported the children by selling jewelry and conducting other small business activities. To extend the family's resources, Braganza lived with her grandmother. Braganza's educational trajectory was unusual for a woman—although she finished grade school and some high school in the Philippines, she left for the United States at age sixteen. Luckily for her, she had an uncle on her mother's side who had first come to the United States in 1903 and who wanted to fund an education for one of his young relatives. Braganza competed with her cousins to get this financial help, winning out over two older male cousins. She arrived in Seattle in 1930, chaperoned by a Filipina teacher named Alpina Zamora, who was looking for employment in the United States. Braganza went to Broadway High School and then enrolled at the University of Washington and Seattle College (later called Seattle University).

As Braganza's story suggests, the contradiction of being both an American colonial traveling to the metropole *and* an immigrant person of color in an American West economy that was segregated by race, class, and gender was part of the regular lived experience of Filipina/os in the first decades of the twentieth century. How they negotiated that contradiction, particularly through education, forms an important part of their experience. . . .

Because of colonialism, the educational experience was somewhat different for Filipina/o Americans than for other groups. The first-generation experience was the central focus for the Filipina/o American community in the pre–World War II era, particularly because many Filipina/os, like Braganza, came explicitly for education and utilized the American public school system as a continuation of education they had received in the Philippines. While members of the immigrant generation in other communities also sought education and went to school, much of the educational experience in the American public school system was directed at the second-generation members of most Asian American communities. Furthermore, because the great waves of Filipina/o migration came during times of tight restrictions on other groups, the demographics of these communities by generation varied considerably. Filipina/o college students encountered primarily second-generation Japanese American and Chinese American university students in the late 1920s and early 1930s. The Filipina/os' different identities and opportunities, as structured by generation, also shaped their experiences in school as well as in the job market.

In addition, particularly because those coming from the Philippines were mostly male, student demographics tended to be extremely gendered. Although some educational opportunities were open to women, the bulk of resources were usually directed toward the men, since both Philippine and American cultures emphasized male privilege. Thus, as a woman, Braganza represented the exception more than the rule. The fact that she required a chaperone indicates that women were far more constrained in their mobility than men. However, Braganza's desire to come to the United States, her reliance on family networks (her uncle), and her travel to public and private educational institutions on the American mainland were characteristic of many in her generation.

Recollections of Colonial Educations

Braganza's decision to go to the United States reflects the sweeping social and economic changes that occurred in the Philippines in the first decades of the twentieth century. Education was the centerpiece of American colonization in the Philippines, and Braganza's cohort were beneficiaries of these policies. One Filipino, "Vic" Bacho, vividly remembered his first day at primary school: "The sight of the children standing at attention when the American flag was raised and singing 'My Country 'Tis of Thee' will always be with me." Half a world away from the mainland United States, Filipina/o children were diligently learning to be good "Americans." Historian Renato Constantino has commented on the inculcation of American culture: "The new Filipino generation learned of the lives of American heroes, sang American songs, and dreamt of snow and Santa Claus." As a class marker, education offered the possibility of upward mobility to ambitious Filipina/os, with the promise of clerical or even professional work at the end of their time as students. The American system, however, was not the first colonial education in the Philippines; Spain had already instituted educational opportunities prior to U.S. rule. Indeed, Jose Rizal, a famous Philippine nationalist hero, first received education in Spain like many of the elite of his generation. He would later travel to the United States, eventually returning to the Philippines to emerge as a political leader.

Students in the first decades of the twentieth century encountered a rapidly shifting political terrain. In his study of Manila before World War II, Daniel Doeppers discusses the changes brought about by the exit of the Spanish administration, the modernization and consequent restructuring of the economy, and the expansion of social mobility across previous class and ethnic divides. Increased American markets for Philippine goods, better transportation facilities, and new economic and financial policies further increased the speed of development.

Importance of Education

Under American colonization, education was a key vehicle in the restructuring of Philippine society. Education followed militarism in the Philippines and was actually conceptualized within a larger system of American domination. As a result, colonial education typically reinforced class privilege and maintained colonial objectives. During American rule, educational opportunities were opened through a national system of public primary schools, promoting change particularly at the rural and barrio (village) level. In this period, colonial education was more accessible than ever before, particularly for men. Although education had been available under the Spanish government, the American system promoted greater access and emphasized a technical and academic curriculum. Within the first ten years, public schools were set up on the primary level in most barrios, on the intermediate level in the *poblaciones* (principal barrios) of municipalities, and on the secondary level in the provinces. Leo Aliwanag remembered, "Gradually they had high schools and then colleges and universities." In Manila, new institutions included an arts and trade school, a nursing school, and the University of the Philippines. To provide teachers for this new system, hundreds of Americans were brought to the Philippines, largely on the transport *Thomas*, earning them the name of the "Thomasites." Other educators were Americans who had remained after the war and become teachers throughout the Philippines.

A Stratified System

Physical location, family background, and gender affected one's ability to secure an education. During its heyday in the early twentieth century, the *pensionado* and *pensionada* program, which sent government-sponsored students to study in the United States, also reflected these social biases. By and large, most of these students came from positions of class privilege, especially because prospective *pensionada/os* were required to be high school graduates. Initially, the Filipino governor and the American school superintendent from each province chose the candidates. Later, the *pensionada/o* program set up examinations for prospective students. Other students were chosen by "special sponsors" such as the Jockey

Club or tobacco and sugar interests. A final twenty-five students were chosen by Governor William H. Taft, whose emphasis on the privileged was clear. As William Alexander Sutherland recalls in his memoirs of the program: "In the telegram of instructions prepared for the Governor to sign was written, 'Each student must be of unquestionable moral and physical qualifications, no weight being given to social status.' The Governor, more realistic than I, scratched out the word 'no' before the word 'weight.' He saw the importance of this, particularly with those first boys going over." The initial *pensionada/os* embarked on their journeys to the mainland United States in 1903, when roughly one hundred students were sent to California. They first attended high schools in southern California, then went to summer school the following year in Santa Barbara. The irony of their position as colonials was underscored in August 1904 when they spent a month at the Louisiana Purchase Exposition in St. Louis. In this celebration of American nationalism, they spent one month in the Philippine Reservation, acting "as guides in the exhibition halls and as waiters in the mess hall," presaging the position of many Filipina/os as native informants and service workers. [writes historian William Alexander Sutherland] The year 1907 saw the highest number of *pensionada/os* being sent abroad: 186 Filipina/os. The *pencionada/o* movement lasted roughly from 1903 until 1910, when most of those who had participated returned to the Philippines. In addition to the *pensionada/os*, other Filipina/o students traveled overseas, especially those from privileged backgrounds.

Hence, the American colonial education system was arranged in tiers. As students ascended the academic hierarchy, they also drew closer to the regional centers, as well as to Manila. However, the pinnacle of colonial education and the mark of the highest prestige was study in the United States.

Filipino Laborers Face Discrimination and Violence

Mae M. Ngai

In this selection author Mae M. Ngai describes the lives of Filipino laborers on the West Coast in the 1930s. By this time, approximately 56,000 Filipinos were living in this area—a number ten times greater than that counted in the 1920 census. Most of these immigrants were single, male, and under thirty years old. The majority worked as migrant farmers, but others found work as waiters, busboys, and janitors. As Ngai writes, these Filipinos faced hostility and violence from white Americans that sometimes led to large-scale race riots. Although people at that time believed the anti-Filipino sentiment arose from white workers' anger that Filipinos were willing to work for lower wages and fears about job competition, Ngai argues that the problem was more complicated. She writes that many white Americans viewed Filipino men as "oversexed" and feared that they fancied white women. Eventually, laws were passed that Filipino-white marriages were illegal. Ngai is an assistant professor of U.S. history at the University of Chicago.

In California, Filipinos, along with Mexicans, became the mainstay of migratory agricultural labor. By 1930 Filipinos comprised 80 percent of the asparagus workforce in the Sacramento River delta region and a major share of the lettuce workforce in the San Joaquin Valley. Living conditions in Filipino labor camps were poor. Although they were noted for their cleanliness, bunkhouses and cabins were of poor construction and severely overcrowded. During the winter, when there was no work, Filipino laborers repaired to the cities. In the early 1930s the Filipino population in Seattle numbered

Mae M. Ngai, "From Colonial Subject to Undesirable Alien: Filipino Migration in the Invisible Empire," in *Impossible Subjects: Illegal Aliens and the Making of Modern America*. Princeton, NJ: Princeton University Press, 2004, pp. 103–15. Copyright © 2004 by Princeton University Press. Reproduced by permission.

only a few hundred during the summer but over three thousand during the winter. For young men seeking education and adventure in America, life was difficult and often lonely. Many regularly sent remittances home. Not a few returned with a college degree or with enough money to buy a piece of land but—as in most immigrant experiences—the majority never did.

Racial violence against Filipinos took place as early as 1926 in Stockton, California. In 1928 in Dinuba, in central California, a gang of white youths attacked Filipino laborers in the company of local white girls. In November 1927 a group of whites expelled Filipino laborers from the Yakima Valley in Washington. An apple grower who had hired eleven Filipino workers brought them to the Sunnyside jail for "safekeeping" after he learned that whites were "en route" to his ranch to "deport" Filipinos. An estimated five hundred Filipino workers left the area that month after white residents threatened to attack them.

Violence in Washington

The following year saw more violence in central Washington. In September 1928, white mobs drove three hundred Filipinos from Wenatchee. A "committee of citizens" met two buses transporting Filipinos to apple growers in Cashmere and "escorted" them out of the valley. Filipinos already working in Cashmere wired Pedro Guevara, the resident commissioner representing the Philippine government in Washington, D.C., that they could not leave the area because they had no funds and that local authorities ignored their appeals for protection. In October, Filipinos reported to Guevara that eight men in Yakima were mobbed. These first incidents of anti-Filipino violence were strikingly similar to the riots that drove Asian Indians out of the state's small lumber and farming towns in 1907–1909.

The eruption of anti-Filipino violence took some people, including officials at the Bureau of Insular Affairs, by surprise. It seemed that throughout the twenties most white Americans had barely noticed Filipinos. Bruno Lasker, who studied the Filipino problem in 1930, could not recall a single article on Filipino migration in a popular periodical prior to 1928. Before 1929, he added, none of the national organizations concerned with immigration or social welfare showed interest in Filipinos. The Philippine colonial project had long faded from the public's attention; both the pensionados and post-World War I migrants who came to the mainland were largely invisible to white Americans. Lasker believed that Filipinos who had arrived in the early 1920s, "students and workers, boys and men . . . for the most part full of hope, and ambition, accustomed to meet life's hardships as they come, trustful— perhaps a little childlike in their simplicity . . . made a good impression [on Americans]. They were not, of course, particularly noticed so long as their number remained small."

Besides the rapid growth of the Filipino population on the West Coast in the late 1920s, however, the reasons for anti-Filipino hostility were less clear. Authorities worried that they knew very little about Filipinos. They did not even know how many Filipinos were in the country. In 1928–1929 the California Department of Labor, the Bureau of Insular Affairs, and the American Council of the Institute of Pacific Relations each commissioned studies to gather facts about Filipino population on the mainland and to adduce the causes of anti-Filipino feeling.

Contemporaries quickly came to the conclusion that job competition was the chief cause of conflict. Yet that conclusion was not supported by the actual patterns of employment and racial conflict. The majority of Filipinos worked in agriculture as migrant farmworkers. If Filipinos competed with other ethnic groups for farm work, it was not with whites but with Mexicans and, to a lesser extent, with Japanese, South

Asians, and Koreans: one contemporary described the competition among migrant workers of color during the late 1920s as "cut-throat." By the 1920s there were few native white Americans in California agriculture, especially in fieldwork; most whites had jobs in packing sheds or as ranch foremen. During the middle and late 1920s, when commercial agriculture burgeoned in California, employers often sought white labor but found it scarce. "Whites won't turn a hand to menial labor during good times," stated a manager of an employment agency in the Imperial Valley.

Filipinos Did Not Compete with White Workers

White farm laborers were often itinerants from other states. Some regularly worked the migrant circuit, mainly picking and packing fruit, but others, according to a labor specialist in the San Joaquin Valley, worked only a few days or a week at a time—"enough to buy gasoline and move on." Growers gave them the "best picking fields" and separate camps "away from foreign labor," but such privileged treatment was not always enough to instill loyalty in the workers. They "leave and even take the tents with them," said one farmer. Growers also complained that whites made poor workers. They said whites worked too slowly and could not pack fruit properly. Turnover was high. They were difficult to supervise. "You can't tell a white boy anything," said one farmer.

Nor did Filipinos compete with white labor in manufacturing or in other urban industries. Filipino employment in hotels and restaurants in Los Angeles and other cities was confined to menial occupations, such as kitchen workers, dishwashers, pot washers, janitors, housemen, and elevator operators. Here, the established workforce comprised African Americans and white women. These workers may have resented the entrance of Filipinos into hotels and domestic occupations, but they were neither the constituency of organized labor nor the active participants in anti-Filipino riots, which took place in rural areas.

In 1928 the California Building Trades Council charged that Filipinos were "forcing their way into the building industry, many of them working as engineers, painters, electricians, carpenters' helpers, and laborers." This claim was also largely unsubstantiated. According to [researcher Bruno] Lasker, Filipinos were confined to unskilled construction jobs and did not compete with white skilled workers. In general, Lasker said, Filipinos were excluded from industrial employment. The few exceptions were in sawmills and box factories. But here, too, Filipinos were hired in unskilled jobs or for seasonal work. In Oregon, Filipinos worked in sawmills only as temporary extra hands.

Moreover, although labor unions complained that Filipinos undercut the wages of white workers, they did not support Filipino workers' struggles against wage discrimination. For example, in 1927 a Stockton box company hired Filipinos at 35¢ an hour when the wage for common labor had previously been 40¢. When they learned that they were paid at a lower rate, the Filipino workers walked out on strike. However, the union that represented skilled workers was prohibited by its constitution to allow Oriental membership, and the skilled white workers in the factory did not join the strike. In another instance, Filipino sawmill workers in Montesano, Washington, struck successfully for higher wages in 1924. Roman Simbe, a leader of the Filipino club that led the strike, recalled, "We shut down one mill, and then another mill. . . . Filipinos alone put up the strike. We shut [the company] down."

Filipino farm laborers also demanded wage equality. In 1928 asparagus workers in the Stockton area elected representatives, who petitioned the asparagus growers with their demands. "Filipino workers intended and always do intend to uphold and EMULATE the STANDARD OF AMERICAN WAGES," they stated. In 1930, Filipino lettuce workers in Salinas struck to protest a wage reduction from 40¢ an hour, the traditional rate, to 35¢. During the late 1920s ethnic labor organizations formed in areas of Filipino concentration throughout California, North of the San Joaquin Valley, in coastal areas from Santa Barbara to Monterey, and in the Imperial Valley. These unions were sometimes organized by Filipino labor contractors, with whom growers negotiated wage rates and other conditions of work.

Filipinos were sensitive to the charge that they undermined whites as cheap labor and believed that by refusing to work for lower wages they might diffuse the hostility against them. The asparagus workers noted that only by "emulating" American wage standards could Filipinos "prove themselves loyal and true to the American most precious TRADITION, thereby becoming [the] most desirable types of people required to remain and live in this country, beyond reproach." Indeed, while the growers who hired Filipino labor praised them for being good workers—they considered Filipinos to be dependable, fast, and physically suited for stoop labor, and found dealing with labor contractors convenient—they also complained that Filipino workers refused to work for less than 40¢ an hour.

Despite Filipinos' efforts for wage equality, anti-Filipino sentiment found violent expression. During the fall and winter of 1929–1930 at least thirty incidents of racial violence against Filipinos took place on the Pacific Coast, including two large-scale race riots and several firebombings. Contemporary observers almost always described the perpetrators as "itinerants," "hoodlums," or "loafers." The first major riot took place in Exeter, in the San Joaquin Valley, in October 1929. Itinerant Italian workers harassed and attacked Filipinos at a local carnival, the latter having brought local white girls to the fair as their dates. For several weeks white men molested or provoked fights with Filipinos on the streets of the town, attacking them with clubs and slingshots made with wire. At the end of the month a mob of two to three hundred whites visited every ranch in the area where Filipinos were employed, demanding their dismissal and destroying the Filipinos' and the growers' property. They destroyed thirty thousand trays of fruit at one ranch and burned a barn and ten tons of hay at another. The sheriff did little to stop the rampage: evidence that later surfaced suggested that he had joined in with, if not led, the vigilantes. Throughout the fall, crudely written signs appeared in Santa Clara and Mountain View: "get rid of all Filipinos or we'll burn this town down" and "work no Filipinos or we'll destroy your crop and you too." In the San Joaquin Valley, a Filipino labor camp in Dinuba was firebombed. Similarly, in Arvin, a "committee" of "loafers" presented growers with warnings and petitions and fired shots at the Filipino laborers' bunkhouses. Filipino labor contractors in the valley insisted on carrying guns in the fields to protect their men.

Yet, curiously, despite the agitation against Filipino employment, the white laborers who attacked Filipino farmworkers often did not actually want the jobs in question. Nor did the trouble appear to derive from anxieties caused by the Depression, which had just begun. Through the late 1920s a labor shortage existed in California agriculture, and whites in rural areas generally had no trouble getting work, despite their reputation for being difficult and unreliable, and the 1929 harvest season was no different. E. J. Firebraugh, whose ranch in Exeter was destroyed by rioters, said, "Nobody [was] suffering for jobs when trouble occurred. Plenty of work doesn't eliminate the possibility of trouble."

A more complicated set of problems, then, seems to have existed. At one level, the riots did express anxiety among whites over job competition, even if it was more imaginary than it was real. White migrant farmworkers who had traditionally worked the fig and apple harvests in Pajaro Valley regarded the increase in the number of Filipinos in the adjoining Salinas Valley's lettuce fields with apprehension and suspicion. The Filipino newspaper the *Torch* pointed out, "The lettuce is a new product in the Salinas Valley. No white men thinned lettuce before the Filipinos. Work in the lettuce fields is very hard." Once the Depression started, Filipinos became the target of resentment among unemployed white workers, for whom Asiatics were familiar and convenient scapegoats, even if they did not want the same work. . . .

Racial Hostility

[T]he reaction of white Americans to the acculturation of Filipinos was similar to the unsettled response of nineteenth-century Americans to acculturated Native Americans, or that of the English to their anglicized colonial subjects of India, whose partial resemblance threatened to mock, even as it mimicked.

Unlike the English, however, white Americans had available to them an avenue for denying the acculturation of their brown-skinned imitators. Because American culture was racially segregated as well as hybrid, white Americans could deny the "American-ness" of Filipinos by ascribing to them attributes that derived from racial representations of African Americans, especially those that depicted black men as sexually aggressive. In fact, this idea neatly bridged the construction of Filipinos as backward savage tribes in the Philippines and the appearance of contemporary, acculturated Filipinos in the United States.

The identification of Filipinos with Negroes was not new. During the Philippine-American War, American soldiers commonly referred to Filipinos as "niggers," which was a familiar epithet that was applicable to all uncivilized, dark-skinned peoples. The racial icon assumed a gendered dimension as early as 1904 when, at the Louisiana Purchase Exposition, a group of white Marines assaulted uniformed Philippine

Scouts—the "most advanced Filipinos"—whom a group of white schoolteachers from St. Louis had offered to escort through the fairgrounds.

Critique of Filipino Sexuality

By the late 1920s the most common complaint against Filipinos, in addition to their alleged displacement of white labor, was that they fancied white women. . . .

The notion that Filipino men were oversexed was commonplace. Their sexuality was linked to their primitive development: references to Filipinos' "childlike" nature undergirded claims of both labor docility and sexual promiscuity. . . .

These racialized sexual representations of Filipino men and fears of race-mixing fueled the anti-Filipino riots in Watsonville, California, in January 1930. Local white youths and Filipino laborers had clashed and fought on the streets on numerous occasions in the late 1920s. As in other towns, the conflicts usually involved Filipinos dating whites, including teenaged girls from local families. In early January 1930, at the urging of Judge D. W. Rohrback, the Northern Monterey County Chamber of Commerce passed a resolution calling for the exclusion of Filipinos from the area. In an interview in the *Watsonville Evening Pajaronian*, the judge declared that Filipinos were "little brown men attired like Solomon in all his glory, strutting like peacocks and endeavoring to attract the eyes of young American and Mexican girls." He believed that the worst part about the Filipino was "his mixing with young white girls from thirteen to seventeen. He gives them silk underwear and makes them pregnant and crowds whites out of jobs in the bargain." Filipinos, the judge added, were "just ten years removed from a bolo and breechcloth. . . . Fifteen of them will live in one room and content themselves with squatting on the floor eating rice and fish."

The judge's language offended the Filipino community. The Filipino Federation of America in Stockton held a mass meeting of three thousand people. The meeting passed a resolution stating that the judge's "malicious and very sweeping [charges] deeply wounded the feeling of all Filipinos; such criticisms phrased in a gross and insulting language being false, unjust and personal in nature." They resolved that Filipinos in the region would "present a solid front for a most vigorous protest" and "show . . . that the Filipinos have self-respect and [are] endowed with humane attributes enjoyed by other people." . . .

The Filipino press in Stockton defended the right of Filipinos to date local women. Angelo Cruz, a Filipino businessman, asserted that the taxi dance hall served a legitimate social purpose, owing to the absence of Filipino women in America; moreover, he said, Filipino men were "much more considerate and respectful toward American girls than the Americans are themselves." . . .

Antimiscegenation Statutes

The conflict over interracial marriage played out in the legal arena as well. Using law to police sexual relations between Filipinos and whites was difficult because the racial classification of Filipinos was legally ambiguous. California's antimiscegenation statutes, which were written in the nineteenth century, prohibited marriage between "white persons" and "negroes, mulattoes, and Mongolians." During the 1920s, U.S. Webb, the state attorney general, argued that Filipinos were "Mongolian," and some county clerks refused to issue marriage licenses to Filipino-white couples. But the courts often disagreed, citing ethnologists that classified Filipinos as being of the "brown" or "Malay race," and not of the "yellow race." In 1933, the Los Angeles Superior Court ruled that Salvador Roldan was "Malay," not a "Mongolian," allowing his marriage to Marjorie Rogers, a "Caucasian." But the court, undoubtedly aware of the race riots attending the Pacific Coast, noted that it ruled only on the law and urged the legislature to align the law with contemporary "common thought." Later that year the legislature amended the antimiscegenation law to explicitly include "members of the Malay race" within its scope. It also retroactively voided and made illegal all previous Filipino-white marriages, a particularly vindictive measure that echoed Attorney General Webb's revocation of South Asian's naturalized citizenship after the *Thind* decision in 1923.

Thus anti-Filipino hostility was a site where ideas about gender, sexuality, class, and colonialism intersected in violent ways and, moreover, informed the construction of the racial identity of both European and Filipino migrants.

The Anti-Filipino Riots of 1930

Emory Stephen Bogardus

In the 1920s the influx of Filipino laborers into the fields of California aggravated tensions with white Californians who were suspicious of newcomers whom they perceived as a threat to their economic security. Some whites also believed "racial purity" would be compromised if Filipinos were freely permitted to date and marry white women.

In Watsonville, California, in 1930 a white mob stormed a dance hall and attacked the Filipino patrons with guns and rocks. The riots continued for a second day, resulting in the death of Filipino farmworker Fermin Tobera. In this excerpt from his 1930 sociological study of these events, Emory Stephen Bogardus documents the events that led up to the Watsonville riot as well as its consequences. He describes a series of Anti-Filipino resolutions that declared Filipinos as disease ridden, promiscuous, and detrimental to the California economy. Racism and anger escalated into a series of violent riots in which Filipinos suffered greatly. Bogardus was the past president of the American Sociological Society and a pioneer in the field of sociology. He was the author of more than twenty-four books, including Immigration and Race Attitudes *(1928). Bogardus died in 1973.*

Within the last two years [since 1928] a number of anti-Filipino demonstrations have occurred on the Pacific Coast. Each succeeding one has been increasingly serious. The conditions that lead to riots have been spreading and becoming more aggravating. . . .

Emory Stephen Bogardus, "Anti-Filipino Race Riots: A Report Made to the Ingram Institute of Social Science of San Diego," San Diego: Ingram Institute of Social Science, 1930.

Anti-Filipino race riots which began in the state of Washington in 1928, occurred at Exeter, California, in October, 1929, and at Watsonville, California, in January, 1930. Both the American and Filipino newspapers have carried extensive reports. At first these reports were sometimes inflammatory but they contained a wide range of facts and interpretations thereof. A few investigations have been made. The disturbances have reached the courts and sentences have reached the record books. In addition to having access to extensive published materials, the writer [Emory S. Bogardus] visited Watsonville in March, 1930 and secured first-hand accounts. These materials were obtained a few weeks after the riots had taken place and hence represented calm and dispassionate judgments; they were particularly valuable because of the time element that had elapsed and because many of the persons concerned were able to view the riots more or less objectively.

The writer obtained first-hand data on the grounds concerning the race riot which has attracted to date more attention, excitement, and discussion than any other of its kind. These data complement well that which has already appeared in print. The comprehensiveness of the first-hand data is shown by the variety of sources from which the data came. The following classes of people were consulted in securing these materials: (1) unskilled wage-earners who view the Filipinos as labor competitors; (2) business men with whom the Filipinos trade; (3) business men with whom the Filipinos do not trade; (4) ranchers who employ Filipino laborers; (5) idealistic citizens, such as pastors and teachers, who stand for spiritual and civic progress; (6) Filipino "stoop" laborers; (7) Filipino labor contractors; (8) Filipino leaders who are intensely loyal; and (9) Filipino leaders who are loyal but also cosmopolitan in viewpoint. . . .

The Buildup

Before the rioting actually started, three factors had come into the open which help to explain the situation that was culminating. (1) A few cases of Filipinos had been brought into court of the justices of peace of Pajaro township, and into the county court at Salinas (of Filipinos living in the Watsonville district). The offences were usually "reckless driving" of automobiles.

(2) On January 10, 1930, there appeared newspaper accounts of a set of Resolutions passed in Pajaro (adjoining Watsonville) by the Northern Monterey Chamber of Commerce and written it is stated by the justice of peace of Pajaro township. The article in the *Pajaronian*, appeared under a double column, first page headline which read: "Resolution Flaying Filipinos Drawn by Judge D. W. Rohrback." The article began as follows: "Coming out square-toed and flat-footed in an expression on the Filipino question, the Northern Monterey Chamber of Commerce adopted a resolution Wednesday night (January 8) designating the Filipino population of this district with being undesirable and of possessing unhealthy habits and destructive of the wage scale of other nationalities in agricultural and industrial pursuits." The article continued: "When interviewed this morning Judge Rohrback said the move of the Monterey Chamber of Commerce was but the beginning of an investigation of a situation that will eventually lead to the exclusion of the Filipinos or the deterioration of the white race in the state of California."

The charges made against the Filipinos in this Resolution were as follows: (1) Economic. They accept it is alleged, lower wages than the American standards allow. The new immigrants coming in each month increase the labor supply and hold wages down. They live on fish and rice, and a dozen may occupy one or two rooms only. The cost of living is very low, hence, Americans cannot compete with them. (2) Health. Some Filipinos bring in meningitis, and other dangerous diseases. Some live unhealthily. Sometimes fifteen or more sleep in one or two rooms. (3) Intermarriage. A few have married white girls. Others will. "If the present state of affairs continues there will be 40,000 half-breed in California before ten years have passed,"—is the dire prediction.

Anti-Filipino Resolutions

The Resolutions included the following statement about sending the Filipinos home: "We do not advocate violence but we do feel that the United States should give the Filipinos their liberty and send those unwelcome inhabitants from our shores that the white people who have inherited this country for themselves and their offspring might live." It is evident that the Northern Monterey Chamber of Commerce did not speak for other Chambers of Commerce for the Resolutions contained the following challenge: "Other Chambers of Commerce have probably passed resolutions endorsing the use of Filipino labor as being indispensable. If that is true, better that the fields of the Salinas Valley should grow into weed patches and our wonderful forests be blackened." These and similar statements speak for themselves regarding the impassioned tone of the Resolutions.

Upon the publication of the Resolutions sensitive Filipino leaders promptly replied. A four-page pamphlet entitled "The Torch" appeared within a few days from Salinas. It contained a detailed reply to the Resolutions, by a member of the editorial staff of the *Three Stars*, Stockton, California. It questions vigorously the truth of a number of statements in the Resolutions and replies sharply to the insinuations of others. It questions the Resolutions when they say that boats are arriving on the Pacific Coast with "thousands" of Filipinos and asserts that no boat has come with more than 500 Filipinos and that many come with none. The Resolutions are quoted to the effect that the Filipinos are but "ten years removed from a bolo and a breechclout." If this is true, then it is asked: "Would you not feel proud to have 'emerged' from 'bolo and breechclout' and after ten years be a respectful citizen?" If the Filipinos live under bad housing conditions, why not report "the case to the State's Building Inspector? Unhealthy? Ring the Health Officer of the State. Don't sit and cry like a Job." Unemployment is charged to the increased use of machinery and to the entering of industry by women. "To discuss the Filipino diet is stupid. Each nation has a particular diet. . . ." To the charge in the Resolutions that "the Filipinos form partnerships and buy good cars and roll along the highways like Solomon in all his glory," the *Torch* replies that the critics "should be glad that the Filipinos, instead of sending their honest-earned money to the Islands" spend it in cars, tires, gasoline and repairs, leaving therefore the dollars in the United States. The statement in the Resolutions that 75,000 Filipinos had recently held a convention in Los Angeles is declared to be preposterous, and the work of an alarmist, for the total Filipino population of California is less than 75,000; moreover all the Filipinos from all over the state could scarcely come together at one time. Such a gross exaggeration, it is contended, indicates that the whole Resolutions are unreliable. The tone of the two articles in the *Torch* closely parallels the tone of the aforementioned Resolutions. Both have inflammatory characteristics.

Filipino Reaction

A few days later, January 19, a mass meeting of 300 Filipinos was held in a hall at Palm Beach, a few miles west of Watsonville, according to a half page paid advertisement in the Watsonville evening newspaper. As indicated by the statements in this article the reactions of the Filipinos to the Pajaro Resolutions had now reached the state of formal group action. Sober thought had supplanted the first emotional reactions. After summing up the criticisms levelled at the Filipinos by the Pajaro Resolutions of January 8th, a carefully thought out reply was given point by point, by a Filipino leader, whose ideas were carefully expressed. The document was couched on the whole in dignified not alarmist terms, as illustrated by the following statement: "We simply want, for the sake of the reading public and the American people in general, to clarify matters and seek out the truth. Ultimately we want to co-operate within our possibilities in solving this problem." Incoming Filipinos, it is asserted, "go into the fields of work where the workers are essentially Filipinos—such work as thinning and cutting lettuce, sugar beets, cutting asparagus, planting and cutting celery, planting garlic, picking grapes, etc. In the above mentioned work one can hardly find a white laborer. . . . It is true that there are fields of work wherein the laborers are mostly whites and are being invaded by Filipinos, but I do not see why they should not, provided they do not receive lower wages."

Low wages are accepted by other people than the Filipinos, by the Mexicans, for instance, it is declared. Low wages have existed in entire districts of California before any Filipinos arrived. Therefore, to blame low wages upon the Filipinos is not to delve into the whole economics of the question of low wages.

On January 11, 1930, a new angle to the race situation in and around Watsonville developed. A small Filipino club leased a dance hall from two Americans at Palm Beach (four or five miles west of Watsonville), imported nine white dance hall girls, and set up a taxi dance hall for the Filipino members. Definite rules of propriety were apparently maintained. The American owners of the property stated that the Filipinos conducted their dances in more orderly fashion than did many American groups who had leased the dance hall property. But the idea of Filipinos dancing with white girls (no matter who the latter were) incensed white young men of Watsonville, and they determined to break up the procedure. As one white person said to the writer: "Taxi dance halls where white girls dance with Orientals may be all right in San Francisco or Los Angeles but not in our community. We are a small city and have had nothing of the kind before. We won't stand for anything of the kind."

Demonstrations Begin

On Sunday, the 19th, the anti-Filipino demonstrations began and lasted until the early hours of Thursday morning, the 23rd. Early Sunday afternoon it is said "that several machine loads of American youths went out to the resort (the dance hall at Palm Beach), but were barred by deputies hired to guard the place." Later that evening several fights occurred on the streets of Watsonville between Americans and Filipinos. On Monday evening, the 20th, the disturbances continued. "Possibly 200 Americans formed Filipino hunting parties, running in groups from 25 to over 100 persons." On Tuesday evening, the 21st, "a mob (of white men and boys) attempted to storm the Palm Beach premises. Word had been passed among the boys of the town that a mass meeting of the Filipinos was to be held at Palm Beach. The boys were aware that several white girls were living on the premises and working in the dance hall there. This fact infuriated them and at eleven o'clock last night full thirty machines, filled with flaming youth," went to Palm Beach, but were met by the owners of the beach resort who held them at bay with guns until "shortly after midnight" when the sheriff, deputies, and constables arrived and "made short work of the mob." Before the arrival of the officers there was some shooting but no one was seriously hurt.

Escalating Violence

On Wednesday evening, the 22nd, the rioting reached its climax. Violence developed into destroying property, beating Filipinos; and finally one Filipino was killed. "Forty-six terror-stricken Filipinos beaten and bruised, cowered in the City Council room. . . after being rescued from a mob of 500 infuriated men and boys who, being robbed of their prey, shattered windows and wrecked the interior of the brown men's dwellings." Further light on the rioting is given: "To the accompaniment of pistol shots, clubbings and general disorder . . . it is believed that 700 trouble-seekers, armed with clubs and some firearms, attacked Filipino dwellings, destroyed property, and jeopardized lives. The most serious rioting occurred on the San Juan road in Pajaro about 10 o'clock. . . when a mob estimated at 250 men entered several Filipino dwellings and clubbed the occupants."

Then came the fatal shot, and the ending of the rioting. A headline and an opening sentence tell the story tersely: "Wild Rioters Murder Filipino in Fourth Night of Mob Terror," and "Mob Violence in Watsonville is ended." A published account reads: "Near midnight a carload of rowdies drove to the ranch (Murphy) and began firing into it. The unfortunate men (or boys) trapped like rats were forced into a closet where they huddled and prayed." One of the Filipino boys, Fermin Tobera, did not follow the others. The next morning, "it was discovered that a heavy bullet, tearing through the walls and a door of the bunkhouse had pierced Tobera's heart."

The better elements of the city became disturbed by the extremes to which the rioting was going. A special editorial made a strong plea as follows (in part): "After the disgraceful scenes of last evening local authorities should come to the conclusion that patience has ceased to be a virtue and that strenuous measures should be adopted to prevent any further demonstrations of that character.

"It is anything but inspiring in this year of our Lord, 1930, to witness a mob of some 400 or 500 individuals attacking a dozen or so frightened Filipinos, rushing into their houses, dragging them out, beating them up, and then wrecking or damaging their domiciles. That is not Americanism."

An Appeal to Stop the Violence

These words are followed by an appeal to save the reputation of the city from the adverse reactions that were being created. The editorial continues: "As it is now, this town has been blazoned over the United States as being the scene of race hatred and violent demonstrations against a race so numerically weak, in our midst, that they are powerless to offer any resistance to the violent treatment given them."

A double-headed request follows, first to the business men and second to the mob leaders. "The business men of this town should awake from their lethargy and in mass meeting assembled, make it known in no uncertain terms to these mob leaders that their conduct is not approved. A word to the members of that mob. We again ask you, as we did yesterday, what do you expect to accomplish by these demonstrations? You are injuring your own cause. Your conduct is offensive to all right-thinking citizens."

Somewhat belatedly the leading citizens of Watsonville came to the rescue of the reputation of the city and of the Filipinos. The headline in the *Evening Pajaronian* summed up part of the reactions: "Volunteer Deputies Bring Welcome Peace to Turbulent Town" The American Legion, the Rotary, the Kiwanis, and other organizations took action in support of law and order, and of protection for the Filipinos.

The *Evening Pajaronian* of the 24th reports that seven (white) boys were brought into the court of the justice of the peace of Pajaro township for preliminary hearing on the charge of rioting. At the hearing a total of eight boys were bound over to the Superior Court of Monterey County. The justice is quoted as stating that he hoped "with all his heart that the judge of the superior court would be lenient in handling their cases as he did not consider them criminals." On February 17, six of the eight youths pleaded guilty at Salinas for attacking Filipinos. On February 25th, the eight were sentenced to serve two years in the county jail. Probation was granted four. The other four were sent to the county jail for thirty days; then put on probation for two years, during which time they must keep away from pool halls, abstain from intoxicating liquors; they must never molest Filipinos and on the other hand they are to lead sober, industrious lives. At the inquest over the body of Fermin Tobera it was decided that the person who had fired the fatal shot was unknown.

After the Riots

Within a week after the rioting, the chairman of the California Athletic Commission "announced a ban on Filipino boxers on all programs in the state." Protests were immediately made by American promoters. Even in Watsonville an American audience in March applauded the suggestion that the Filipinos be allowed again to appear in boxing matches with Americans. One promoter, addressing a crowd in Watsonville, is reported as saying that the fight game could not be run in Watsonville if the Filipinos were not allowed on the cards. "The crowd was unanimous in roaring approval to the proposition of having some real fast Filipinos on the next card."

But how did the Filipinos conduct themselves throughout the riots and afterwards? A few at the start were evidently inclined to fight back. A few argued vigorously. An editorial writer in the *Watsonville Register*, says; "A disposition to too much argument on the part of the Filipinos is apparent at this critical period. Their advisers should caution them against it." When the rioting was at its worst the Filipinos did not fight back. If they had done so, the riots would doubtless have turned into massacres. From out-side cities, such as Stockton and San Francisco there were two reactions: first, of those who were incensed and excited. A few evidently responded to a communist circular calling upon the Filipinos to rise up and fight for justice.

Filipino Community Leaders

Second, there were the Filipino leaders who advised caution. Under date of January 24, a mass meeting of Filipinos in the nearby city of San Jose was reported. The purpose was "to prevent the Filipinos from resorting to violence. Filipinos will be asked to rely on the police for protection if necessary, rather than taking the law into their own hands." Early in February the Filipino Emergency Association came into existence in San Francisco for the specific purpose of "preventing participation by Filipinos in any further California race rioting with whites." The additional statement appeared in the *Pajaronian* that the Filipinos "showed co-operation with local authorities by avoiding conspicuous places where they would mingle with whites." When the trial of the Watsonville youths took place, the Filipino Emergency Association sent letters from San Francisco to the district attorney and others urging clemency "in the interest of good will and harmony between Americans and Filipino citizens."

Filipinos all over the United States and especially in the Philippines were greatly disturbed by the rioting in Watsonville and particularly by the killing of one of their number. In general the reactions took the form of increased demands for independence of the Philippine Islands. In Manila particularly did excitement run high. Demands for independence were coupled with public remonstrances against the mistreatment of Filipinos in the United States. February 2 was observed as "National Humiliation Day" by several thousand Filipinos "who gathered for services protesting against recent anti-Filipino demonstrations at Watsonville, San Francisco, and San Jose, Calif." The adverse reactions in Manila broke out in March in a school strike involving perhaps six thousand high school pupils because of asserted insults directed against the Filipinos by one of the teachers. When the body of Fermin Tobera, slain at Watsonville, arrived in Manila, "thousands of Filipinos took part in orderly demonstrations." Tobera's body lay in state for two days. Tobera was declared a national hero and for a time at least occupied a pedestal along with Jose Rizal, the national hero of the Philippines. A member of the Philippine Legislature was quoted as having said at the burial services that the bullet which killed Tobera "was not aimed at him particularly; its principal target was the heart of our race," and Tobera was said to have been slain by a mob of "bloodthirsty Americans." The reverberations of the Watsonville riots were heard around the world. Feelings were aroused to a fever pitch; ill will was multiplied; Filipino-American race adjustments were made infinitely more difficult. Here and there, however, Filipinos pointed out that not all Americans were vicious, bloodthirsty, or even unfriendly. Here and there ill will and rioting were admitted by Americans as hindrances rather than helps in settling racial conflicts.

Family Networks and Religious Customs

Fred Cordova

In 1983 American historian Fred Cordova assembled a collection of documents, essays, first-person accounts, and anecdotes about life by the first wave of Filipino immigrants, sometimes known as the "manong" or "older brother" generation. In this selection from Cordova's collection, a variety of Filipino Americans from all walks of life discuss the family networks they established in the United States in the first half of the twentieth century. He writes that Filipinos had a much broader idea of what constituted a family than white Americans. For Filipino Americans, the family included godparents and close friends who came to be regarded as "uncles" and "aunts." This extended family system provided a great deal of support for the Filipino immigrants struggling to make it in their new country.

Fred Cordova is the founding president of the Filipino American National Historical Society, and is a second generation Filipino American. Cordova is currently a manager of news services at the University of Washington, Seattle.

When a Filipino American was born into this world—on the U.S. side of the Pacific Ocean—that Pinoy infant belonged to a family of potentially no less than one hundred members, beginning with father and mother, brothers and sisters, uncles, aunts and cousins to the 'nth degree equally on the paternal and maternal sides . . . and, if that new-born had been very fortunate, also to have been blessed with grandparents, granduncles and grandaunts.

Those were just the "blood" relatives. The "nuclear" family circle also internalized "in-law" uncles and aunts, etc., etc.

Fred Cordova, "Family Network," in *Filipinos: Forgotten Asian Americans*, Dubuque, IA: Kendall/Hunt Publishing Co., 1983, pp. 133–44. Copyright © 1983 by Demonstration Project for Asian Americans. Reproduced by permission.

Our parents more or less raised us under strict discipline like they did in the Philippines, and at that time and with my father also with my mother, you did not argue. You did not explain. Their word was final.—Angel Bantillo Magdael, Stockton, California

Daddy is storeboy ... plantation store. He look me, come to my house and promise marry. Nobody take care of me. That's why I gonna marry. No more big wedding. My uncle bring me by the kind. No church ... judge only. April 28, 1925 ... first child born. I got eight children.—Ambrosa Balmores Marquez, Kauai, Hawaii

1931 I went home and got married. I came back because I got no money. I have a job ... save some money and with the help of the captain, we went to the immigration. He stood for. I get my wife. She came here 1937.—Sinforoso Laigo Ordona, Seattle

The Extended Family

The family network went beyond white traditional ideas of what comprised a family to the broader Filipino American concept of the "extended" family.

A chief factor developing the "extended" family was the Pinoys' distinctive "compadre" system. There were godparents, sponsors, for the baby's baptism, the young child's reception of First Communion, the adolescent's confirmation and the young adult's marriage—all couched in Catholic ceremonies of various sacraments designed for the growing person's spiritual benefit. Godparents or "compadres" and "comadres" became, in fact, spiritual fathers and mothers. This religious kinship became irrevocable. The child became "related" as well to the godparents' children, they having become godbrothers and godsisters in a familial relationship sometimes growing closer than that between cousins.

I have two godparents. When my mother died, love was extended from these two families. To this day, I am very close to them. One family lives in Reedley, California, and the other

here in Sacramento. Therefore, all my roots are in the valley and from these families came much of my thoughts, feelings and inspiration.—Ignacio Ladrido Balaba, Jr., Sacramento

The baby's family was strengthened by other kinds of alliances. Strong bonds became even more intimate among close friends, who for years had been almost like brothers and or sisters to either parent or both. This close friendship started when parents and their friends had been living in the same barrio (village), town or province in the Philippines.

By 1930, my son was born so we moved . . . because we would like to have our own apartment. Then we move again and we got a flat . . . six, seven rooms, including the kitchen, the dining room and the living room. So, there is four bedroom. . . . We asked our townmates to come and share with us also. So, they were nice enough to help us and they come. We rented the room to them. That's how we get by.—Magdalena Rillera, San Francisco

Family life in our home was always lively. By day, the house was alive with the coming and going of the Bolima children, our cousins and friends. By evening, people would begin calling on my father. Generally, they were his countrymen. . . . They had been referred to him for help of different sorts.—Sonya Bolima Fujioka, Seattle

Friendship Bonds

Tight friendships likewise began in the U.S. when Pinoys had started to work at the same jobs or when they had joined the same clubs. They also lived together for years. These friendships were the result of Filipino American adults sharing good and bad times together in America. These close friends then became the baby's "uncles" and "aunts." When some of these single "uncles" or "aunts" had married, their spouses, too, became part of the family circle and were regarded as an "uncle" or "aunt."

We didn't have that many permanent people but we had always people dropping in and there was always a bedroom

available. Everybody, even if they weren't related was always "uncle" or "aunt."—Santiago Abastilla (Jim) Beltran, Juneau, Alaska

Throughout the years in the U.S. the Filipino American interpretation of "family" went beyond traditional concepts as held by white and other Americans. Likewise, the Filipino American acceptance of who had become family members transcended all beliefs about family kinships as followed by most Americans. It has been no wonder that non-Filipinos had thought all Pinoys were related to one another. More significantly, the support system within the Pinoy family network has been short of being unbelievable.

I matriculated to U.C.L.A. on a scholarship. However, that summer my brother, Nicky, went to New York. Paul was married to Jovy and he was in Santa Ana taking care of his own family. My sister, Becky, left for the Philippines. Consequently, no one was here to take care of the family. So I gave up my scholarship, my chance to go to college and took care of the family.—Julian Ebat, Oxnard, California

I raised the son of my sister-in-law. My wife's sister is married to Filipino . . . I raised him as my own. We were living together. I was the sole support of all the family.—Rufino Corpuz Dumo, Detroit

I was born in Stockton, California, September 21, 1926. I have my brother . . . myself and sister . . . I remember when my mother ran away when I was little . . . I was left with my dad. My mother left on a horse. My dad had no one to care for me at the time he was working, so he left me with Mr. and Mrs. Todtod. They raised me for a little while.—Connie Amado Ortega, Seattle

Many of the young Filipinos at that time would look up to a family because they felt that a family was closer together than a single man. Mom would wash their clothes for them, iron their clothes for them.—Terry Rosal, Stockton

Sometimes I own my car with my brother or my cousin. We fill up the car when we go . . . share each other. We share all the time. Even the groceries we split. Whatever we spend, we divide it up. Even when we work, contract job, whatever we make, we divide it equally.—Fred Bello Castillano, Stockton

Marriage and Family

After World War Two, families began to increase among Filipino Americans because of immigration to augment those which had developed, especially on the mainland, since the first decade of the twentieth century. Marriage unions between two Filipino partners were hard to come by during the 1920s, 1930s and 1940s in stateside U.S.A., which had reported a sex ratio of fourteen brown men to one brown woman or one thousand four hundred Pinoys to one hundred Pinays. Pinoys married Pinays but these Filipino American unions were not enough to provide a permanent base for Pinoy communities. What did result was a large number of interracial marriages to supply that solid foundation in the Pinoy communities.

Thus, the Pinoy children of these marriages and unions have not all been brown-skinned. These Pinoys have been identified as White, American Indian, Chicano, Alaska Native, Black, Hawaiian, Puerto Rican, Chinese, Japanese, Hispanic and other combinations of ethnicity. Such an identification has been half-right. These Pinoys have claimed such mixed parentages . . . including Philippine regional mixtures.

My mother almost had a fit when I was marrying an Ilocano. Can you believe that . . . because I'm Visayan. . . . I was fifteen. I know how to take care of a home. I know how to take care of my husband. I know how to cook even though I put sugar in everything. But I took care of my family and I raised them. . . . My oldest brother and my second brother was married to white women. They didn't feel the impact of it near as much as their children did. Their children felt the impact.—Hyacinth Camposano Ebat, Oxnard, California

They work in the cannery here. . . . They were married to these native women. . . . They had their family.—Mateo Ylanan, Ketchikan, Alaska

If they did want to marry, because there weren't many Filipino women, it would be white girls or Mexican girls that was close to Filipinos because they work shoulder to shoulder with them in the field.—Alfonso Perales Dangaran, Fresno, California

(My wife) is young, got many sister and all kinds of brother. . . . Went back to the United States, use to write. I kept writing and then she come to New York . . . Got married about 1928. She's Danish.—Luis Reyes Acuzar, Long Beach, California

They don't allow intermarriage in Portland. Yet, we go to Vancouver, Washington, where they allow intermarriages.—George Pimentel, Portland, Oregon

I'm Polish . . . We got married in '34 and had a hard life. My mother disowned me. Old people are prejudiced. This is our life. . . . You can't buy a home because you are not an American citizen. We rented the first nine years and then we bought a house, two-family flat. My sister and her husband lived downstairs. We lived upstairs and after five years my mother came to live with us and my husband was her favorite son-in-law. . . . You talk to these American women that I'm married to a Filipino. They're going to give you a lot of ". . . nigger lover!" American people say "nigger lover" to the American woman.—Sophie Bilbat, Detroit

I saw her. She's on . . . Shibo, Japan . . . Married in 1957, Oregon. We together 1953. Long time. Many (Filipinos) married to Japanese. All in the merchant marine. All of them meet in Yokohama.—Bruno Ibabao Tapang, Seattle

Everything had to be on the secret side. They just hated white women that was married to a Filipino. It was just as low as you can get. I knew him when I was fourteen . . . I wouldn't tell my mother but I'll tell him. He would come and see what

I was doing. He was the father, sweetheart and husband-image to me. He didn't know that I loved him. . . . (Our neighbors) wouldn't speak to me. They'd say all kinds of rude things to my mother. I realize now that she suffered a lot on account of me, of us. I cried bushels of tears. . . . It was a sad thing but I've been happy. We had all these fifty-five years of it now.—Hazel Simbe, Aberdeen, Washington.

My wife is an American. I have five children and twelve grand-children . . . happily married for forty-eight years . . . married in 1933.—Leandro dela Cruz, Chicago

The permanence first-generation Filipino Americans had sought but which had been elusive was attained through their having families and children, second-generation Pinoys, who were U.S. citizens by birth.

My folks were not citizens, so they could not buy a house. They bought the house, but the house was under my name and my brother, George, and still is. If you were not an American citizen, you could not own a property. They could never own a farm. They were just laborers, working in the agricultural field.—Terry Rosal

As late as 1942 when we moved to the south part of Stockton, my mother came to buy this house. The people across the street told my mother that they would pass a petition around to keep us out of here. At that time, my mother could not own property. Filipinos were not allowed to own property. They put it in my name.—Angel Bantillo Magdael

They could own the property after the war, not before the war. If you are not a citizen, you cannot buy it. You could buy it through your children because they are citizen.—Magdalena Rillera

The Filipino American family with its immediate and extended members has been racially and ethnically rich with a diverse background. No matter how many kinds of racial bloodlines have run through the veins of Filipino Americans, they have been Pinoy, because of strong family ties. Such a legacy has been what the first-generation has been attempting to teach the succeeding generations.

One good thing about the Filipinos, though. I don't think we were in the breadline. We never see anybody who was on the breadline because, like I said, we share.—Felipe Lucas, San Francisco

CHAPTER 2

COMING TO
AMERICA

The Second Wave of Filipino Immigration

Filipino-American Military Service in World War II

Alex S. Fabros

In 1941, at the beginning of World War II, Filipinos, considered U.S. nationals, were called to serve in the military by President Franklin Delano Roosevelt. Roosevelt authorized the creation of the 1st Filipino Battalion on March 4, 1942, according to military historian Alex S. Fabros. This regiment, based in California, consisted of Filipino expatriates, Filipino Americans, and white Americans. In this selection Fabros describes the formation of this battalion and the challenges faced by Filipino American soldiers. Fabros notes that many of these soldiers returned to the U.S. mainland with Filipina brides, to form a new generation of Filipino Americans. Alex S. Fabros, a Filipino American, is a military historian for the California State Military Museum.

The circumstances of World War II, brought about the constitution of various ethnic American military units. Among them was the 1st Filipino Infantry Regiment, consisting of a blend of Filipino expatriates, Filipino Americans by birth, and white Americans. The 1st Filipino Infantry Regiment, humble in its beginning, however, dramatic in the challenge of the mission it had to fulfill, to finally retire with honors earned through individual sacrifices, that resulted in a brilliant and illustrious history.

The American people, by Act of Congress in 1935, promised the Filipino people their full independence by the year 1946. The new Philippine Commonwealth government proceeded to assume the task of a new democracy, and in doing so, had established a militia, with the help of General Douglas MacArthur, then assigned as Military Advisor by the United States government.

Alex S. Fabros, "California and Second World War: California's Filipino Infantry," The California State Military Museum, www.militarymuseum.org/Filipino.html. Reproduced by permission of the author.

Just six years into being formed, the Philippine Army, with the American trained Philippine Scouts, and the American Armed Forces stationed in the Philippines, came under attack, and within a few months found the invading Japanese Military forces solidly entrenched on Philippine soil. The following year American and Philippine forces stubbornly fought to defend the islands, only to surrender to overwhelming conditions in early 1942. Freedom and democracy was not to be earned easily. Many Americans and Philippine troops refused to accept surrender. Some escaped to eventually return with allied forces. Others remained behind and began a crusade against the enemy.

By the time America entered World War II, there were over a hundred thousand transplanted Filipinos in Hawaii and the United States mainland. The impact of the unprovoked attack brought on the call for volunteers for our armed forces. Thousands of Filipinos answered the call to arms, which began a new page in Filipino heritage. These Filipino American units played a tremendous role in the liberation of their former homeland. . . .

Formation of the 1st Filipino Battalion

Thousands of Filipinos had petitioned for the right to serve in the U.S. military immediately after December 7, 1941. On January 2, 1942, President Franklin Delano Roosevelt signed a law revising the Selective Service Act. Filipinos in the United States could now join the U.S. Armed Forces and they were urged to volunteer for service. President Roosevelt quickly authorized the founding of a Filipino battalion, which would be organized for service overseas. It estimated the number of available Filipino volunteers between 70,000 and 100,000.

The 1st Filipino Battalion was formed on March 4, 1942 and activated in April 1 at *Camp San Luis Obispo*, California. Lieutenant Colonel Robert H. Offley, who had served in the Philippines and spoke passable Tagalog, volunteered to be assigned to the unit as its first commander. He assumed command in April 8, 1942. The War Department also directed Philippine army officers and soldiers who were stranded in the United States at the start of the war to report to the unit. An unusual point is the designation of the unit. Previous Filipino units in the U.S. Army had been designated "Philippine" such as the Philippine Scouts. All units raised in the U.S. during the war were designated "Filipino." Also, it would not be until the end of the war that the Filipino military units would carry the designation "Infantry" in their title although their regimental colors from the very beginning were displayed on a blue field, the traditional color of the infantry branch of the army.

A number of wounded Philippine Army and Philippine Scouts had escaped to Australia from the Philippines on board the USS Mactan in December 1941. Some remained in Australia to form the nucleus of what would eventually become the 1st Reconnaissance Battalion, but the rest were sent to the United States for further medical treatment. These men eventually reported to the 1st Filipino Battalion.

Contrary to popular belief, the 1st Filipino Battalion was not established as a result of the American policy of social segregation. Only Filipinos who volunteered for assignment to the unit were sent to it. Many others, such as Eutiquio V. "Vic" Bacho, served with distinction in "American" (white) units in the European theater of operations during the war. . . .

Many of these men were part of the migratory labor force that followed the harvest season along the Pacific Coast, from California farms to Washington fruit orchards and Alaskan fish canneries. Others had lifted themselves by their "bootstraps" into college and took the limited white collar jobs that were open to them. Having endured white America's racism, these men knew how to adapt to rapidly changing situations. They relied upon one another for strength. Communal living on the farms permitted them to adapt quickly to military life.

Leading Filipino musicians of the time made up the regimental band. Sergeant Urbano Francisco composed the regimental marching song, "On to Bataan;" but it was not uncommon for the men to march to the strains of the latest "boogie woogie" or "swing" song.

By the end of May 1942, the strength of the 1st Battalion had reached over 2,000 men. The unit was ordered to Salinas, California where it became the 1st Filipino Infantry Regiment on July 13, 1942. The Salinas rodeo grounds which had just been vacated by Japanese Americans who had been sent to remote concentration camps, housed the regiment. Because of the strict anti-miscegenation laws then in effect along the U.S. west coast, many of them married into other non-white ethnic groups. Among the most popular group to choose from were Japanese women, the daughters of Issei immigrant farmers. The manongs must have impressed the Japanese women greatly to cause many of them to reject the strong Japanese dislike of "Gai-jins" (foreigners). C. Sales wrote in the January 29, 1934 issue of the Philippine Mail of a young Romeo-and-Juliet couple. A certain Silvestre, a Filipino, and Alice Taneka, a Japanese, were engaged to be married. When her family tried to force her to break off their engagement, they committed double suicide.

Anti-Asian Racism

In April 1942, Lieutenant General John L. Dewitt, Western Defense Commander, ordered the Japanese on the West Coast into concentration camps. Miguel Ignacio, secretary of the Filipino American community of San Francisco, called attention to several American-born Japanese women, citizens of the United States, who had Filipino husbands, and Filipino-Japanese children who were U.S. citizens by birth. Despite the efforts of the American Civil Liberties Union, Dewitt ordered the women and children to spend the duration of the war in the internment camps. Many of these Filipino husbands went on to serve in the 1st and 2nd Filipino Regiments, defending the nation whose racist policies held their families hostage.

In September 1942, the first group of qualified Filipino enlisted men was sent to the Officer Candidate School, Fort Benning, Georgia. Upon graduation, they were commissioned second lieutenants in the U.S. Army. The War Department planned to have Filipino officers eventually command the majority of the combat units in the 1st and 2nd Filipino Regiments. Events beyond the control of the military planners in Washington, D.C. intervened to prevent this from being fully implemented.

So many Filipino volunteers came from all over the United States that the 2nd Filipino Infantry Regiment was formed at Fort Ord, California on November 22, 1942. In January 1943, the 1st Regiment was reassigned to *Camp Beale*, near Sacramento and the 2nd Regiment to Camp Cooke, near Santa Maria. The two regiments were to be joined by a third regiment consisting of Filipinos from the Hawaiian National Guard. However, the Hawaiian Sugar Plantation Association argued successfully with the martial law commanders in Hawaii that not only was cheap labor on the plantations necessary to support the war effort, the Filipinos in Hawaii were forbidden by the Tydings-McDuffie Act from going to the continental U.S. The men could not leave the sugar plantations and were paid substandard wages for the duration of the war. This would have serious consequences in 1946 when the militant Filipino labor unions shut down the islands until their demands for wage increases and better working conditions were met.

As a result of a May 1942 Gallup Poll showing strong support for the naturalization of Filipinos, the Filipino Naturalization Bill was passed. Pinoy GI's were urged to apply for U.S. citizenship. A mass swearing in of over 1,000 soldiers was held at Camp Beale on February 20, 1943. Many of the men, however, resisted becoming citizens. T-5 Julius B. Ruiz stated that although he had lived in the United States for many years and was now serving in the U.S. Army, his goal was to liberate his country, the Philippines. By the time the 1st Regiment left for the western Pacific in May 1944, over half of the men in the unit were U.S. citizens. . . .

Challenges and Milestones

Before the 1st Regiment departed for the western Pacific in May 1944, Colonel [Robert H.] Offley [first commander of the 1st Regiment] had a major dilemma on his hands. Even though his regimental chaplains were prepared to perform marriage ceremonies between the Filipino soldiers and their white girlfriends, the strict anti-miscegenation laws in California prevented the men from applying for marriage licenses. Colonel Offley solved this by sending his soldiers and their sweethearts to Gallup, New Mexico on chartered buses that soon came to be called the "honeymoon express."

Meanwhile in New Guinea, the 1st Regiment quickly integrated its first batch of replacements consisting of Filipino Americans from Hawaii. Colonel Offley gave Lt. Col. Leon Punsalang, a West Point graduate, command of the 1st Battalion. This was the first time in the history of the U.S. Army that Asian Americans commanded white troops in combat.

The 1st Regiment landed at Tacloban, Leyte on February 7, 1945 and fought the Japanese troops on Samar. In one combat action, the regiment reported killing 1,572 Japanese soldiers while five of its men were killed in action. In May 1945, the regiment began operations in northern Leyte in the Villaba-Palompon sector where it fought heavily for the next two months, registering an average of 40 Japanese killed and 32 captured a day. . . .

[After the war] The families of many of these men had given up hope of ever seeing their sons and brothers return from the land of broken promises and dreams. The manongs [Filipinos], who were despised by white America, and yet were needed in the American farms and fisheries, returned to their Philippine homeland as heroes. When the men reported back to the 1st Regiment on Leyte, many brought with them new brides. The Filipino soldiers took advantage of Public Law 271: The War Brides Act of December 28, 1945 and Public Law 471: The Fiancees Act of June 29, 1946 to marry Filipina women. Colonel William Robert Hamby, who had replaced Colonel Offley, established a "tent city" for the married couples. Before its expiration on December 31, 1953, [m]any manongs took advantage of the War Brides Act [of 1945] and returned to the Philippines to marry. These families became the nucleus of a new generation of Filipino Americans and invigorated the Filipino American community in the United States.

Filipino American War Brides

Carolyn Jung

During World War II many Filipino and non-Filipino soldiers who were stationed in the Philippines met and married Filipina wives. On December 28, 1945, the U.S. Congress passed Public Law 271, known as the War Brides Act. This legislation, along with the Fiancees Act of 1946, granted Filipina wives of American veterans and soldiers permission to immigrate. The following article, published on the fifty-first anniversary of the arrival in the United States of war brides from Leyte, Philippines, describes the lives of some of these women. As author Carolyn Jung writes, in the best cases, loving couples started new lives and became part of Filipino communities in the United States. Some women, however, found themselves expected to enter forced unions in order to obey familial wishes. Upon arrival in the Unites States, both willing and unwilling expatriates faced poverty and discrimination. The War Brides Act expired on December 31, 1953.

Carolyn Jung is a journalist who has covered minority affairs and is currently food editor for the San Jose Mercury News.

More than a half-century ago, the chances of Filipino-American men finding wives were dismal. Immigration patterns had created a lopsided situation in which single Filipino-American men outnumbered eligible Filipino-American women 40 to 1. And state laws banning interracial marriage condemned most to lives of unmarried anguish.

Then World War II gave many of these men a chance to serve their country and their heart. The Allied invasion of Leyte, the pivotal battle to liberate the Philippines during the war, also became a defining moment when hundreds of Filipino-American U.S. soldiers met the young Filipino women they would marry.

Carolyn Jung, "War Brides," *San Jose Mercury News*, October 20, 1995, www.ignacio. org/warbride.html. Reproduced by permission.

With cultural divides and an average age difference of 20 years, these unions often didn't start out smoothly. But they endured. And they formed the foundation of communities here, particularly in the Bay Area, where there are 261,273 people of Filipino ancestry, the second-largest concentration in the country.

These couples settled in the Bay Area to labor on farms, work in the burgeoning electronics industry and keep alive traditions from their native land.

Most of the men have since died, and many of their wives have remarried. But the women say they always will cherish the memories of their first love.

A Loving Union

This year would have been Victor and Gregoria Fangonilo's golden wedding anniversary had he not died four years ago at the age of 76. His Palo Alto wife still remembers fondly how they met on Leyte when a cousin dragged her to a GI camp to return some uniforms an aunt had altered.

"While I was standing outside a tent, I saw so many Filipino officers. I couldn't believe they were all in the Army. They started whistling at us," she said, blushing even today.

Victor, an Army supply sergeant, walked out of the tent and introduced himself. He was 33; she just 17.

One day while she was minding her cousin's store, Victor dropped by. He told her he was going downtown, but he was headed the wrong way. Later, she realized he had really come to see her. Indeed, after they had met, he had bet his sergeant $20 that he would marry her.

Even after being sent to another island, he wrote every week. "They were love letters so beautiful that I had to read them many times," she said.

Much to her dismay, she fell in love. She was scared because she'd heard that American soldiers who married Filipino women deserted them when they were transferred back to the United States. But that didn't happen in this case. The couple married in the Philippines eight months after they met.

Like many war brides, Gregoria didn't want to leave behind the world she knew in the Philippines to come to the United States. But in 1947, a year after they married, she was on a ship with 177 other Filipino war brides headed for San Francisco.

While many Filipino men emigrated to the United States in the 1920s and 1930s for work and educational opportunities, Filipino women were not encouraged to make the journey, said Alex S. Fabros Jr., executive director of the Filipino American Experience Research Project at San Francisco State University.

That left a U.S. population imbalance just as the war's devastating effects in the Philippines resulted in the death of many young men and a surplus of single young women, he added. Complicating matters were this country's anti-miscegenation statutes. The colony of Maryland passed the first law against interracial marriage in 1661, aimed at preventing black-white marriages. Eventually, such laws existed in 38 states. In 1905, they were extended to prohibit marriages between whites and Asians.

Only in 1948 were such laws declared unconstitutional in California, and not until 1967 were all such statutes finally done away with in the United States.

The immigration of these war brides had a profound impact on California, Fabros said. Before 1940, there were 1,502 Filipino women in the state. A decade later, that figure had jumped to 5,141, he said.

Similarly, in 1940 there were 5,327 married Filipino-American men in California. By 1950, there were 17,660, Fabros said.

"It gave us our communities here because the women wanted to settle down and start families," Fabros said.

"Through cooking, dances and storytelling, the women also helped preserve the culture."

A Forced Union

While the Fangonilos' marriage was a mutual decision, Sally Panis, 69, of San Jose found herself in a far different predicament.

Her uncle, who worked in a GI camp, introduced her to Valentine Sabado, an Army gunner. Panis was 19. Sabado was 40.

"My mother was three years older than him," she said of her widowed mother. "I told him to marry my mother."

But her uncle had other plans. "My uncle said if I didn't marry him, he would shoot me," Panis said. "He told me that twice. I was scared."

So she married Sabado in 1947, three months after they met, and she came to the United States two years later.

"I wanted to go home," Panis said. "For three months, I cried. He kept saying I would get used to it."

She did, growing to love her husband's kindness and even temper. He died in 1957 of a brain hemorrhage while she was pregnant with their fourth child. A week after he was buried, the baby was born. After being on welfare for a few years, she got a job as a hotel housekeeper that she kept for 26 years.

Poverty and Discrimination

The war brides' lives often were hard. Pacita Partolan Caballes, 71, of Palo Alto came to the United States in 1947 after two years of separation from her husband, Army Cpl. Ramon Partolan, while he saved enough money to pay for her passage.

Caballes had been so poor in the Philippines that she owned only one dress and wore banana leaves for shoes. Seeing how destitute the family was, Partolan brought them Army bread, rice and vegetables.

Although she hardly knew him, her mother urged her to marry him because he had been so kind. Life in the United States wasn't much easier for a while. For a time, as they raised flowers with the Fangonilos, the couple lived in a house with no water and ate wild mustard for food. Even when they had saved enough to buy a nice house, they faced discrimination from real estate agents who steered them to East Palo Alto when they wanted to live in Palo Alto, Caballes recalled.

But she always had faith, she said, largely because of her husband, who stood by her as they raised six children before he died of cancer in 1985 at age 77.

"Coming here as a war bride was a risk," Caballes said. "I didn't know what would happen to me. But I realized that if you have a husband who is good and supportive, there's no problem that can't be solved."

Reparations for Veterans

David A. Pendleton

In 1998 David A. Pendleton was among the many speakers who testified at a hearing before the Veterans' Affairs Committee of the U.S. House of Representatives regarding Filipino veterans of World War II. Throughout the 1990s several attempts were made to pass legislation that would have granted veterans' benefits to Filipino servicemen. The Filipino Veterans Equity Act failed to win passage in 1995 and again in 1997. In this hearing, advocates for the aging population of World War II vets argue that time is running out to rectify a mistake made by not granting GI benefits to a population that served honorably and in large numbers in a time of war.

In December 2003, President George W. Bush signed a bill providing health care at Veterans Administration facilities for Filipino American veterans living in the United States. In March 2005 Filipino American veterans lobbied for house and senate bills HR 302 and S. 146, collectively known as the Filipino Veterans Equity Act of 2005, which would restore full military benefits and pensions to Filipino American World War II servicemen. These bills are currently stalled in committee.

In the following testimony, Pendleton, the grandson of a Filipino American veteran, discusses the injustice of denying Filipino servicemen due recognition for their war service. David A. Pendleton is a former member of the Hawaii House of Representatives. He is also an attorney and Seventh-day Adventist minister.

Before the Veterans' Affairs Committee, House of Representatives United States Congress, The Honorable Chairman Bob Stump and Honorable Members of this Distinguished Committee:

David A. Pendleton, Statement before the House Veterans' Affairs Committee, United States House of Representatives, Washington, DC, July 22, 1998.

My name is David A. Pendleton. I am a state legislator from Hawaii. More specifically, I am a Republican member of the Hawaii House of Representatives, where I serve in the Minority Caucus as Whip.

On behalf of the Hawaii State Legislature, and particularly the Filipino Caucus of the Hawaii House of Representatives, Aloha and thank you for inviting me to testify today. I also extend the sincere appreciation of thousands of Filipinos from my home state of Hawaii for this Committee's gracious scheduling of this important oversight hearing.

It is clear that there are many pressing issues before the House Veterans' Affairs Committee, and so your committing time to this issue evidences a recognition of the important contribution of the Filipino veterans of World War II. It is hoped that this hearing will be the first of several significant steps toward genuine equity for our Filipino veterans.

My Grandfather Was a Veteran

Distinguished members of this Committee, my interest in Filipino veterans' issues derives partly from the fact that I am of Filipino ancestry. My late grandfather was born in the Philippines and served in the United States Navy. He was enthusiastically patriotic, not just on the Fourth of July but throughout the year.

He ultimately immigrated to Hawaii and was proud to become an American, proud of the fact that he was a citizen of a Nation committed to high ideals—liberty, justice, equality before the law. I still remember visiting grandfather and hearing him whistle the National Anthem while he shaved in the morning before going to work at Pearl Harbor. He was a civilian by that time, but you'd never know it.

He was also proud of his Filipino heritage and culture. He passed this on to his children and grandchildren. He spoke often of World War II and was ever grateful for General Douglas MacArthur's bravery. My uncle is named Douglas, after the legendary general.

I never mastered the details of World War II military history, but I grasped the themes, the major events, and acquired a sense of the times from my grandfather's account. He hurried over many of the details. Some of these details had to do with the treatment of Filipino veterans immediately following the war.

Misunderstandings and Policy

His position—as I now reflect upon what he said—was that some misunderstandings occurred, some unfairness took place, and some representations were made which were not lived up to. But that was the past.

My grandfather was clear that today's leaders could not rightly bear the guilt of those who had gone before. Decision makers in the present are not responsible for what others did or did not do.

My grandfather did teach me, however, that while we cannot be held responsible for what others have done in the past, we are responsible for what we do in the present and in the future. Perhaps what happened was perfectly legal in terms of technical compliance with the letter of the law.

There are others here much more versed in these matters who will discuss this issue. But even if we assume that what was done was technically legal, viewed in the broader context of history and how we have treated others similarly situated, it is clear that there is not equity for Filipino veterans. Even if the present scheme is perfectly in keeping with the rules, it falls far short of our American ideals.

Full Equity Is Deserved

And this is the difficult part. We can all agree that justice and equity are the goals. We can all agree that justice and equity may require that we do more than we are presently doing, but what are the precise or specific terms? What exactly should be done? What statutory language would effectuate our American ideals with respect to Filipino veterans?

I will not attempt to answer all of these questions during the next few minutes. I have written articles on this issue which were published in local papers in Hawaii—and two of the articles are attached to my written testimony.

My main purpose today is to convey to you my firm belief—and that of the Hawaii State Legislature, as expressed in the House Concurrent Resolution—at the present treatment of Filipino veterans does not afford them full equity. Because I am allotted only five minutes for oral testimony, let me illustrate this contention with two brief points. There are many other points which could and will be made. I will leave that for other testifiers this morning.

Separate and Unequal Treatment

First, there is the issue of naturalization. During World War II, many non-American soldiers were involved in this great conflict, fighting against the powers of conquest, namely, Japan and Nazi Germany. Among the military forces which opposed Japanese and German expansionism were allied troops from other countries. These troops, not unlike the Filipino veterans, fought in conjunction with American forces against a common enemy. They were subsequently afforded the right to naturalization.

Beginning in 1943, naturalization officers were dispatched to foreign countries where they accepted applications for naturalization, performed naturalization ceremonies, and swore into American citizenship thousands of veterans from other countries.

In contrast, the great majority of Filipino soldiers who had fought under the command of American officers were not afforded similarly liberal naturalization policies. The United States withdrew its naturalization officer from the Philippines for nine months and then permitted the law to lapse in 1946, resulting in severely limiting the number of Filipino veterans able to exercise their rights in a timely fashion.

Second, there is the issue of the reasonable and appropriate form of payment of monetary veterans' benefits. While other veterans of World War II (who presently reside outside of the United States and served in a similar capacity as the Filipino veterans) receive the full equivalent value of their veterans' benefits in their home currency, such is not the case for many Filipino veterans. Instead, Filipino veterans receive the equivalent of only half of the dollar value, regardless of whether the recipient resides in the Philippines or elsewhere.

An Issue of Fairness

I could discuss many other issues, but there are others here who will discourse upon such matters at length. I want to emphasize that the Filipino veterans of World War II are not seeking special or extraordinary benefits. They are asking for equal benefits that otherwise would have been accorded to them were it not for the Rescission Act which was alluded to earlier.

Permit me to close by reminding us all of the purpose and goal of the Department of Veterans Affairs: "to care for him who shall have borne the battle."

The United States Congress has an opportunity to effectuate genuine equity for Filipino veterans. Let us today begin the arduous but necessary task of crafting legislation which will assure equity for Filipino veterans.

Let us care for those who have borne the battle.

A Filipina American's Life in the 1950s

Juanita Santos with Yen Le Espiritu

Many Filipino immigrants living in the United States arrived in the 1950s after completing some form of service for the U.S. government in World War II. In this excerpt from an oral history, Juanita Santos describes her experiences as a Filipina immigrant in San Diego in the 1950s. She met her husband, a Filipino American who worked for the U.S. Veterans Administration in the Philippines and married him in 1946. They moved to San Francisco in May 1952, then relocated to San Diego in June of the same year.

Santos, who had trained in the Philippines as a pharmacist, found work in a hospital. In her new position she encountered ignorance and racism and found herself the victim of misconceptions about Filipinos. Santos shares her memories of the Filipino community in San Diego, her experiences as a working mother, and her community activism. Juanita Santos was born on March 30, 1918, in Sarrat, Ilocos Norte, Philippines.

I was born in Sarrat, Ilocos Norte. According to my mother and my aunt, my birth date was March 30, 1918. But in 1952, when I applied for my passport to come to the United States, I discovered that on my birth certificate, my birth date was April 8!

My father and mother were both grade-school teachers. My father died when I was three years old. When I was in the third grade, we moved to Laoag, where Mama and Auntie taught in the elementary school across the street from where we lived. We always lived together in the same house—Auntie, Mama, my sister, my brother, and me. . . .

Juanita Santos, "We Have to Show the Americans that We Can Be as Good as Anybody," in *Filipino American Lives*, by Yen Le Espiritu, Philadelphia: Temple University Press, 1995, pp. 43–51. Copyright © 1995 by Temple University. All rights reserved. Used by permission of Temple University Press.

After high school graduation, I went to Manila and lived in the YWCA dormitory, and took up pharmacy at the Philippine Women's University. At that time, it was an exclusive women's university. I wanted to take journalism but that profession was not considered "feminine" then. When the war came, I had to go home to my mother in Ilocos Norte. Because the guerrilla activities against the Japanese were becoming intense, my mother brought me back to my aunt and uncle, who had evacuated from Baguio to Caloocan, a suburb of Manila, where it was still relatively safe.

Marriage and Emigration

After the war, I met A. B.—who became my husband. . . .

I was twenty-eight and A. B. was thirty-eight years old when we got married [in 1946]. . . . I received my B.S. in pharmacy in 1947.

After that, the Veterans Administration sent A. B. to the Cagayan Valley to be the manager of the USVA [U.S. Veterans Administration] branch office there. I went with him. . . .

In 1952, A. B. quit the USVA and returned to the United States. He came by himself in January. I was taking my master's degree in social work at that time, but I did not finish it because I wanted to join my husband. So in May, I left the Philippines for San Francisco.

When we went out on the day I arrived, the first person whom I saw was a very beautiful American lady with a hat that had flowers all around it, and she smiled at me. In the Philippines, you don't just smile at anybody. But here, she smiled. I thought to myself, "Well, this America must be as beautiful as this lady." When you leave your country, you leave everyone that you love, everything that is familiar. I was feeling so lost. But that beautiful lady, to me, she was America.

Life in San Diego

In June 1952, we came to San Diego because A. B.'s brothers lived here. I did not know what to do with myself, but I knew

I wanted to work. So I went to take up typing and bookkeeping. Then A. B. brought me to see the sisters at Mercy Hospital [a Catholic hospital in downtown San Diego]. He used to work there as a vegetable buyer. He also formed the Filipino American Catholic Society at Mercy Hospital. A. B. was a favorite of the sisters because he was a hard worker and an activist. He would rebel and tell the sisters off. That's what Sister Augustine and Sister Dorothy used to tell me. With the other Filipino boys, it was always "Amen," but A. B. was different.

As soon as we arrived at Mercy Hospital, Sister Augustine brought me to meet Sister Anna Marie, the supervisor of the pharmacy, because A. B. had told them that I had a pharmacy degree from the Philippines. So the sister hired me right away! I was very lucky. Sister Anna Marie was very supportive, very kind to me, but she was a terror to nurses who did not know their medicines.

When our son Michael was born in 1959, we decided that I should stay home and take care of him. It was only when he was in high school that I started working again, but only part-time so that I could be home when Michael was home.

Stereotypes and Ignorance

In the 1950s, most Americans thought that Filipinos just worked in the kitchen. My first week at Mercy Hospital, I was typing the label for one of the prescriptions. And here came a doctor. He asked me, "Hey, do you know what you are doing?" When I gave him the label, he turned to Sister Anna Marie, my sister supervisor, and said, "Hey, Sister, she knows what she is doing." The sister told him, "Of course, she is just as educated as you are." The next thing he said was, "Are there schools in the Philippines?" I was shocked. I shook my finger at him—he was tall, very handsome, blue eyes—and I said, "You know what, Doctor, you are ignorant. Our University of Santo Tomas is twenty-five years older than your Harvard University." And you know what? Since then, my inferiority complex—being short, and very brown, and very Filipino—fell away, because if this educated man is ignorant, what more with the "ordinary" green, yellow, blue man on the street?

Once when I was reading the bulletin board [at Mercy Hospital], a woman came up to me and asked me if I knew how to read. I told her that I did. When she asked where I worked, I pointed to the pharmacy. She apparently did not believe me, because she went to talk to the sister, and when she came out of there, she just looked at me, up and down. But I didn't know that those were prejudices; to me, these people were just ignorant.

Another time, one of the sisters told me, "My child, are you lost? The kitchen is that way." I said, "No, Sister, I work at the pharmacy." At Mercy Hospital, there were some twenty or so Filipino workers in the kitchen. All of them were very nice, devoted family people.

Because of this ignorance, every time there is a Filipino program and I am the master of ceremony, if we have any professional on stage, I will always mention that she is a pharmacist, he is a doctor. . . . The other Filipinos in town used to say that I was prejudiced and that I only recognized professionals. But that was not true. I just wanted to "educate" the other races that the Filipinos are as knowledgeable and cultured as they are. I wanted respect for my people. I wanted to project a positive image of the Filipinos and my native country.

The Filipino Community

When I first came to San Diego, there were very few Filipinos—maybe about one hundred families. We knew everybody. There were a few farmers. There was one Filipino family who owned a big farm in Chula Vista. At that time, their property was worth $250,000. That's a quarter of a million! And these people were not educated; they could hardly speak English. But they got divorced, and they had to sell.

Most of the Filipina women in San Diego in the 1950s were wives of Navy men. There was only one schoolteacher from the Philippines. She was also a GI bride. I was a minority. I was the first one to work at a pharmacy. And you know what, they [the other Filipinos] used to look down on me because I was one of the "educated" ones.

The first time that I attended Rizal Day celebration* sponsored by the Filipino community, I wanted to crawl under a chair. I was not looking down on them, but the people who were on the program did not speak very well, and the program was not the way it should have been. The following years, I waded in, and I helped them because they had to be taught. I shouldn't say they had to be taught, but I wanted to share what I knew, because at the Philippine Women's University, they taught us many things. It was not just books; it included social and civic training and everything.

In 1955, even though I was recuperating from surgery, in my bed I wrote a three-act play about Dr. José Rizal: Part I was the farewell party for Dr. Rizal; Part II was the three Filipino artists in Madrid; and Part III was Rizal writing his last farewell. That year, the San Diego mayor attended the Rizal celebration, and that started the relationship between the Filipino community and the city of San Diego. And we, the Filipinos, became recognized and were respected.

Community Involvement

In the 1950s, because the Filipino community was so small, it was very close-knit. Everyone loved getting together. We came from different regions in the Philippines, but it did not matter. We all spoke Tagalog. I didn't speak Tagalog very well, so I

* A Filipino national hero, José Rizal was accused of inspiring the Philippine Revolution to oust the Spanish colonial regime with his writings and was executed by a firing squad in 1896. Part I of the play refers to the farewell party in Rizal's honor as he left for Spain at the age of 21 to continue his studies; Part II re-enacts a discussion that Rizal had with two of his Filipino friends in Madrid concerning their roles in the impending Philippine Revolution: Part III features Rizal writing his farewell poems while being imprisoned in Fort Santiago.

had to learn it fast. The Filipinos lived downtown, and around us. They were not spread out yet. There was one family in Pacific Beach, three or four in Chula Vista, and later on, maybe after ten years, another family in Linda Vista. . . .

We used to be very, very close. We were one big family. When we had a picnic, Oh, my Lord, everybody would come. Now we don't know everybody like we used to. The Filipino community is so dispersed today—Poway, Mira Mesa, Oceanside, San Ysidro, National City, Imperial Beach. . . .

I am still very active in the community. Right now, I am a member of the board of directors of the Philippine American Community of San Diego County, which sponsors the annual Miss Philippines Pageant. The pageant is to show one and all that Filipinas are beautiful, intelligent, and talented! I am also president of the American Legion Auxiliary of Leyte 625. Because my husband is a World War II veteran, I like to help with their programs. They work so hard to help the veterans and the communities. These involvements keep me from being completely retired.

After more than forty years in the United States, I have gotten acclimatized to the mores of the United States. I see, and I accept. I don't look down; I don't look up. I just accept. But I am Filipino first. When I go out, I don't care what kind of person that I meet, professionals, European, American, or whatever, I have no inferiority complex—or whatever complex.

A Filipina Migrant Laborer Adjusts to Life in the United States

Iluminada Imutan, as told to Janet Shirley

In this selection, Iluminada Imutan compares her life in the Philippines to the radically different conditions she found after immigrating to the United States in 1964. Imutan was unaware that her ailing parents had been working as migrant laborers in San Francisco, and when she joined them, the poor living and working conditions shocked her. Fed up, Imutan and other Filipino laborers joined the Agricultural Workers Organization Committee (AWOC), the group which initiated the Great Grape Strike of 1965. Imutan recalls fondly how Chicano labor leader Cesar Chavez and the United Farm Workers Union joined in the strike and helped Filipino labor organizer Larry Itliong organize the struggle to improve the plight of migrant laborers. Janet Shirley, who recorded this oral history of Iluminada Imutan, is a writer, activist, and member of the New Humanist Writers' Network.

I never knew how good we had it until I came to the United States. Every morning I would go to the beauty parlor and get my hair fixed, I would return home to tell the maid what to cook for dinner. I had a big house. My husband had a nice job selling real estate so I didn't have to work.

I had my group of friends and we would socialize everyday. My biggest worry was to make sure I would get home before my husband arrived for dinner. That's all I would do. That was my life in the Philippines.

Janet Shirley, "Iluminada Imutan, Delano Farm Worker," *Heritage*, vol. 12, issue 2, Summer 1998, pp. 26–30. Reproduced by permission.

A Move to California

In 1964 we decided to move to California. My mother and father were here and they both had been getting sick off and on. Sometimes my daddy would be in the hospital, then my mother. I was worried about both of them and since I am the eldest daughter, I felt that I had to come.

I felt responsible. My mother and father were employed as farm workers in Delano at the time. They petitioned for us to come to the United States. I was already married with three children and actually my husband didn't want to come but I talked him into it. At the time, Diosdado Macapagal was still president.

We arrived in San Francisco at night and drove until we reached Delano. It was then that I discovered that my mother was just living in a one bedroom shack on a farm. The shack was owned by the growers. It had one bedroom and a very small living room. And there we were—five of us plus my parents!

The funniest thing is that my parents lived in a place called "Richgrove" in Delano. So before I came I thought everyone was rich there. But that wasn't the case. It was all farm workers living in a barrio. I was so shocked when I arrived. I asked my parents, "why didn't you tell me you lived like this?"

Disappointment

I was so disappointed! I thought in America everything was push button like I saw in the movies. Maybe it would have been different if we ended up in Los Angeles or San Francisco. But we ended up in Delano. Here I was, coming from a city and ending up in a barrio! It was a big shock.

Delano was like a big grape field. I remember that the grape trestles didn't even have leaves on them when we arrived. They looked like crosses in a cemetery. I thought to myself—"my god, where are the tall buildings?" Everything was like a big field or cemetery.

The worse part is that we had left everything in the Philippines. We sold our house. My husband had left his business. We had nothing to go back to and it would be shameful to go back. Even our relatives had given us a big farewell party in the Philippines—thinking that going to America would be a big thing. Now there was no turning back. I was so disappointed that I cried for a whole week.

Within days we moved out of my parent's house. We had some money because we had sold everything in the Philippines. We bought a house in Delano. In those days it cost about $25,000, but we could only afford the down payment. I still thought that I could get rich.

Cost of Living

When I left the Philippines, the average salary was 4 pesos a day for a professional teacher. The exchange rate was 4 pesos to each dollar. I got so excited when I found out that my parents made $1.10 an hour. I thought, since my parents made the same amount of money in one hour that a teacher makes in a day in the Philippines, I was going to get rich here. I thought $1.10 an hour was a lot. So I told my father that I wanted to work with him in the fields.

My father really didn't want me to do that work. He knew that I had high blood pressure. He told me that the work in the fields was very hot and sometimes while they are working with the grapes they would be sprayed with sulfur or pesticide. But I insisted that I wanted to work in the fields with my daddy. I'm spoiled in that way. Since I'm the eldest I can get my way.

My father used to tell us about discrimination. In Delano there was a movie house. You could not sit on the left side of the theater. That was for white people. There was a certain part of the sidewalk that was only for whites. There were certain restaurants where Filipinos could not go in. They put signs up saying we weren't allowed in.

My father tried to explain the exploitation we faced. He would tell me, "look, we go to the grocery and we only make $1.10 an hour. We have to buy a pound of hamburger. A white collar worker makes $2.50 an hour. But both of us pay the same for the hamburger!"

A Difficult Life

My mother also taught me how hard things were. She taught me that things weren't like they were in the Philippines. For example, here everyone does housework. Even if you are rich, you have to do something in the house. She told me that even [First Lady] Rose Kennedy washed her own dishes.

Farm workers work really hard. They get up just as soon there is light. I had never experienced such work. At that time I didn't realize that farm workers were the most exploited of anybody. And there's lots of discrimination with the growers, especially before the strike.

For example, you would be working in the fields in the summer and there would be no cold water. It gets really hot in the summer. We only had one cup to pass around the water among us. The cup smelled really bad, like old sardines. There were no portable toilets. So what we did, when we wanted to pee was to hide behind grapevine leaves and go there. When I had to go, the other girls would cover me up and I would do the same for them. And you were always in a hurry so no one would see you.

One time I was sprayed in the field. I was picking grapes under the grapevine. The planes would go very low to spray and shoot what looked like smoke out the back. All of us were sprayed with pesticide. This would never happen now, not after we won the strike. Back then, though, they sprayed when they wanted to.

A Lack of Support

Many of the Filipinos didn't have any family with them in California. For many years during the twenties and thirties,

Filipino men were not allowed to marry white or Mexican women and there were no women from the Philippines around. So they lived as a group of single men in a camp. In the winter it would get so cold and they didn't have heating or anything. We would go and visit them and during the strike we would go and feed them.

During the sixties there were lots of Filipinos working in the fields. They worked in the asparagus fields as well as the grape fields. Many Filipinos immigrated here to do labor, and other Filipinos went to Hawaii and Alaska in the 1930's. By 1965, many of these Filipinos were old men.

The Labor Strike of 1965

Anyway, conditions were so bad that we decided to strike. It was a group of young Filipinos that started the grape strike in 1965 under the leadership of Larry Itliong. Larry was the leader of the AWOC [Agricultural Workers Organizing Committee]. He was working in Delano as a grape picker.

He began organizing the farm workers. It was hard though because the growers would bring in truckloads of scabs—mostly illegal Mexican workers. Larry began talking to [union organizer] Cesar Chavez to convince him to join us. Of course, Cesar could not commit right away to the strike. He had to ask his membership first.

So then the Filipinos and Mexicans began to organize as one—side by side on the picket line. Helen Chavez became my friend. Dolores Huerta too. They treated us very well. We were like one family because we were fighting one cause.

I remember Cesar Chavez very well. He was a good man. He cared about everybody—not only Mexicans. He cared about the Filipinos too. Considering that we were very few at the time compared to the Mexican workers, Cesar cared about us just as much. We were just like brothers and sisters in the strike.

During the early part of the strike, I remember there was a train that was going to take the grapes of Delano to another state. We didn't want the grapes to go anywhere. We called them scab grapes. We knew when the train was coming down the tracks. So we laid down on the train tracks to stop it, I was so frightened. But nothing happened and the train didn't move. Finally all the picketers were sent home.

Strikers Versus Scab Workers

I remember one time on the picket line. Helen Chavez, everybody was there. The scabs were working in the field right in front of us. We women strikers were trying to talk to the scab women inside the field. We would tell them, "why don't you join us? It is for your own benefit. If you join, the strike may end soon. Everyone will benefit."

And the scabs were saying: "but we have families, we have to work!" But we told them, "if you have to work, go to another area where there is no strike." Some of these scab women were really nasty. Some of them called us *putas*—prostitutes. But we had to be non-violent.

I didn't understand what they were saying in Spanish so I asked Helen Chavez to translate. She told me: "they are saying we work in the bars at night as *putas*." I got so mad when I heard this that I threw a big clump of mud at them. And then, all of a sudden, all of the women started picking up dirt rocks and throwing them at each other.

When Cesar heard this he got really mad. He pulled us off the picket line. He gave us a sermon that we were supposed to be non-violent. He asked who started the fight, but we all stayed quiet. We told him that the scabs had called us bad names. Cesar told us of course that it wasn't true what they were saying but that we shouldn't react. We just have to stay non-violent.

An Historical Visit

After that we could no longer work on the picket line. All the wives were given different jobs. Some Filipino women went to work in the kitchen of the Delano headquarters, some would handle the mail. I was trained as an accountant.

I remember one day I was in the kitchen at the Filipino Community Hall. I heard that Robert Kennedy was going to visit Delano but I didn't imagine he would visit our Filipino Community Hall. But he came and visited the kitchen and asked me what I was cooking. I opened up the pot to show him a big batch of beans I was cooking for the strikers.

When I saw him come into the kitchen I was speechless. I never imagined I would meet him so directly. Later I would campaign for him in Los Angeles. It was so terrible when he got shot. We farm workers were so sad we couldn't even talk to each other.

Looking Back

I thought when I came to America I was coming to paradise. But I landed in a barrio in Delano. And I thought to myself, "is this America?" Looking back I learned the importance of loving poor people and how to appreciate their work. Here I have learned how to work.

Here I realized how hard it is. Especially when I became a farm worker. When I was in the Philippines I thought I would be better off being in America. I had nannies, maids, a driver, a home. My husband was making good money.

Here everything has been hard. I remember one time I tried to talk my girlfriend into coming to the U.S. She's a beautician in the Philippines, a very successful businesswoman. I told her that she could be successful here.

But she told me, "no thanks Luming, America is yours. You can have it. When I come home at night at least I have someone to cook for me. In America you work outside, and then you come home and work again. You can't even afford to smile there. At least in the Philippines I can still smile."

Perhaps I was greedy to come here. But I was worried about my parents. I knew they were sick and in and out of hospitals in California. I never knew my parents were farm workers before I arrived to the States. And I never bothered to ask before. Maybe they didn't tell me because they were ashamed. Friends who came to visit the Philippines from the States never mentioned my folks were farm workers.

Actually we were quite o.k. in the Philippines. Looking back I realize I had a better life in my country. But I thought that everything in America was going to be like paradise. I thought everything would be automatic. We had a house in the Philippines. My husband worked in real estate. I didn't have to work. But when I came to America I realized that there is hardship here. I had no idea.

There was no turning back after I arrived in Delano. I have a feeling that God sent me here to experience what I have experienced. I didn't recognize the hardship of the poor before. Now I know how important it is to value the work of poor people.

COMING TO
AMERICA

Later Waves of
Filipino Immigration

The Family Responsibilities of Filipino Immigrants

Rhacel Salazar Parreñas

As Filipino immigrants settle in the United States, many rely on both their nuclear and extended families for financial and emotional support. In addition, many Filipino immigrants provide regular financial support to their family members who remain in the Philippines. In the following selection, Rhacel Salazar Parreñas interviews a group of Filipina domestic workers in Los Angeles about their significant financial contributions to relatives living in the Philippines. Many of these women have single-handedly funded education in the Philippines for their entire extended families—Parreñas notes that in these transnational families, single relatives without children take responsibility to help support the younger members of the extended family. Rhacel Salazar Parreñas, formerly professor of Asian American studies and women's studies at the University of Wisconsin, is currently associate professor of Asian American studies at the University of California, Davis. She is the author of Children of Global Migration: Transnational Families and Gendered Woes, *and* Servants of Globalization: Women, Migration, and Domestic Work.

Much like other immigrant groups in the United States, Filipino migrants turn to the family for support against the social and economic pressures that they encounter upon settlement. They use the family in myriad ways. For example, Filipino migrants are known to have preserved various cultural practices to secure the use of the family as a source of support in settlement. . . .

Rhacel Salazar Parreñas, "New Household Forms, Old Family Values: The Formation and Reproduction of the Filipino Transnational Family in Los Angeles," in *Contemporary Asian America: A Multidisciplinary Reader*, Min Zhou and James Gatewood, eds., New York: New York University Press, 2000, pp. 336–42. Reproduced by permission of the author.

[O]ne strategy of household maintenance utilized by Filipino migrants for easing their settlement into the United States . . . [is] the formation and reproduction of the Filipino transnational household. By transnational family or household, I refer to a family whose core members are located in at least two or more nation-states. In such a family, a migrant settles in the host society, while his or her family—spouse, children, and/or parents—stays in the Philippines. . . . [In this study] I rely primarily on interviews conducted with twenty-six Filipina domestic workers in Los Angeles. I supplement this data with interviews that I had gathered with fifty-six domestic workers in Rome and ten children who had grown up in transnational households. Transnational households are in fact the dominant strategy of household maintenance for migrant Filipina domestic workers. Of the twenty-six women interviewed in Los Angeles, twenty maintain transnational households. Of these twenty women, fourteen have dependent children living in the Philippines, one lives apart from her husband in the Philippines, and five are single women whose monthly remittances sustain the day-to-day living expenses of their families. . . .

The Burden of Financial Support

The operation of transnational households rests on the strength of mutual assistance among extended kin in the Philippines. In transnational households, the migrant shoulders the responsibility of providing for primary and extended kin by remitting funds regularly. In fact, not one of my interviewees has failed to provide consistent financial assistance to her family. Notably, most single migrants send remittances to elderly parents on a monthly basis. Only those with relatives (e.g., brothers and sisters) working outside the Philippines do not send money regularly since they are able to share the responsibility of financial support.

Another mechanism on which transnational families rely is consanguineal responsibility, that is, the extension of responsibility to parents, siblings, and even nieces and nephews for those without children. The high level of interdependency in extended families of Filipina domestic workers is first illustrated by the tremendous responsibility women have for their extended kin in the Philippines. Many single domestic workers shoulder the financial costs of reproduction of the extended family by investing in the education of younger generations. While married domestic workers with children usually cover the schooling only of their own children, those who migrated as single women support extended kin prior to marriage. Besides sending remittances to cover the day-to-day living expenses of their parents and other relatives, Pacita Areza and Letty Xavier [two of the women interviewed], for example, covered the costs of the college education of at least four nieces and nephews before getting married in the United States.

> I sent my sisters to school. . . . One finished a degree in education and the other one in commerce. One only finished high school. . . . Until now, I still help my nieces and nephews. I am sending them to school. With one of my brothers, I am helping him send his two children to college. One just graduated last March and one has two more years to go. With one of my sisters, she has two children and she does not have a job and she is separated from her husband. I help her out—I am helping by paying for their schooling. Once all my nieces and nephews are done with their schooling, I can go back to the Philippines. [Pacita Domingo Areza, married with no children, domestic worker in Los Angeles]

> From the start, when I started working in the Philippines, I have helped my family significantly. My nieces and nephews, I sent them to school. . . . One of the first nephews I sent to school is a civil engineer. . . . The second one is a midwife, and the third one is a teacher. The next two sisters are also in education, and they are all board passers. My dreams

have come true through them. Right now, one is in nautical school, and he is going overseas soon. Right now, I have stopped supporting them. Those I sent to school, I want them to be the ones supporting their younger brothers and sisters. They are their responsibilities already. I think I have done my part. (Letty Xavier, married, domestic worker in Los Angeles)

Familial Obligation

Of thirteen migrant workers who at one point had been single women in Los Angeles, five women sent at least three or more nieces and nephews to college. Others provided valuable financial support to their families. Besides subsidizing the everyday living expenses of elderly parents, some purchased the house where their parents and siblings, including those with children, now live and sent at least one younger relative to college. As Gloria Diaz, a domestic worker in Rome with a sister in the United States, explains, they would feel guilty if they did not provide for their relatives in need: "When I don't send money, I feel guilty because my mother is alone, and it is my obligation to help."

Often, the primary contribution of migrant domestic workers to the "kin work" of the extended family is the education of younger generations. In acknowledgment of their extensive support, younger members of their extended family often consider the migrants second mothers. Nieces and nephews refer to them as "Mama" or "Nanay" (Mom) as opposed to just the customary reference of "Tita" (Aunt). For domestic workers, their financial assistance to the family provides them the most tangible reward for their labor. Because of a cultural system based on an economy of gratitude, the immense generosity of migrant workers, especially adult single migrants, guarantees them a well-established kinship base if they choose to return to the Philippines. This economy of gratitude is premised on the value of *utang na loob*, literally, debt of the soul, in which favors are returned with lifelong debt.

A Young Filipina Immigrant Struggles with Family Separation

Roselyn Domingo

New immigrants to the United States face a variety of challenges, including changes and disruptions of family life. In many cases, families are split up for long periods when some members immigrate to the United States while others remain in the Philippines. Roselyn Domingo, the author of this selection, describes feeling anxious and sad when her father left the family in the Philippines to look for a better life in the United States. Domingo and her sister joined their father in the United States a year later, but her brother and mother stayed behind in the Philippines. Within two years, Domingo's father developed cirrhosis of the liver and passed away, and Domingo remained in the United States with her aunt's family. Facing life-changing problems without her father or her mother's presence has proved a daunting task. She states that writing has helped her explore her feelings about being a teenage Filipina in the United States. Domingo was born in 1984 and moved to California from the Philippines in 1992. She is a writer living in Union City, California.

Looking back, I remember living with my family in the Philippines. We went to the park together, and my father carried me on his shoulders as we walked to the playground. He put me in a swing and pushed me, the wind breezing through my hair. Afterward, we had a picnic. My mother fed me, while my father made funny faces to make me smile. All that mattered to me was that I was with my family.

Roselyn Domingo, "Separation Anxiety," in *Yell-Oh Girls!: Emerging Voices Explore Culture, Identity, and Growing Up Asian American*, Vickie Nam, ed., New York: Quill, 2001, pp. 59–62. Copyright © 2001 by Vickie Nam. Reproduced by permission of HarperCollins Publishers Inc.

I was eight years old when I found out that my father was leaving the Philippines to go to America. Determined to provide a better future for his family, he was going to become an American citizen and petition for the rest of his family to come to America. A year later, he was able to send for my sister and me to come to America. Unfortunately, he could not send for my mother since they weren't married yet, and my brother was too young to make the trip alone. Had my brother left the Philippines, too, my mother would have been so lonely with all of her children gone.

Back then I didn't know exactly what was happening. I just obeyed my parents' orders, not realizing that I had left my mother and brother until I was already in the air where clouds were the only objects I could see outside my window. Wondering when I would meet the rest of my family again, I cried so hard that I thought my heart would explode. I couldn't stop my tears from rolling down, and my sister became irritated and angry toward me because of my continuous mourning. I was dolorous without anyone who could comfort me.

After spending some time with my father, he told me that he had to leave us because his work was going to be in Los Angeles. My sister and I had to stay in Union City with my aunt and her family. Every weekend, my father drove from LA to Union City so he could spend time with us. What I regret the most is not cherishing every moment I was able to spend with my father. A year and a half later, he developed cirrhosis, a liver disease caused by excessive consumption of alcohol over a period of years. He went to the hospital for frequent checkups. His condition worsened, and soon he had tubes in his stomach, and had to be careful when moving around. During the roughest times, he would even vomit clots of blood.

One night, my father and I were silently watching television in my room. He kept getting up to go to the bathroom to vomit, so I followed him to make sure he was okay. He vomited pieces of blood on the bathroom sink. I was frightened and worried. My father told me to call the doctor and our relatives. Everything happened so quickly; later, all I could remember was the sound of the ambulance. My relatives joined me and we followed my father to the hospital. He was shaking and he could not even speak to me. I did not know what to do or say to him. I cried, and I prayed for my father's health and safety, but my prayers weren't answered. He died in the summer of 1994. He didn't even live to celebrate Father's Day or to see his children grow up and graduate from school. He was a great person, a loving father, and a devoted husband, but for some reason, out of all the people in the world, he was the one who had to die so soon. I was filled with mixed emotions—mostly rage, denial, and sadness.

My father's body was brought back to the Philippines. My mother couldn't believe that her husband had died. They had so many dreams together. She was on the verge of giving up on the world because she had lost the most important person in her life. She didn't even get to bid my father farewell or tell him how much she loved him one more time. My brother didn't get a chance to spend time with him, either. He thought our father was sleeping when he saw him in the coffin. In spite of my father's funeral, I was glad that my family was finally reunited. I thought that I would be fine as long as I was with them, but I was wrong again. My aunt told my mother that she could take care of my sister and me in America so we could become American citizens in a few years. She said that later we could petition the rest of my family to come as my father had originally planned. My mom felt uneasy, but she agreed with my aunt, and said that this arrangement would be for the best. It was hard letting go, but I knew she left us so that we could have a better future and because she loves us.

It's been seven years since I came to America. My aunt and her family are my second family. My sister is eighteen, and she's applying for American citizenship. It will probably take months or even years until her citizenship papers are fully processed and approved. Right now, all I can do is write to or call my mother and brother. Every two to three years, my aunt arranges a trip so that my sister and I can fly to the Philippines during our summer vacation. I am thankful, but it is not enough. I see my friends and their families living happily together and I envy them. I pray every night that someday I can be closer to my family, but it's getting harder. I am so afraid of losing my family and never living with them again. I seek help but there is no one who can console me. None of my friends know what I am going through and my sister does not bother talking to me about our problems.

The only person who can give me comfort and relief is my mother. She understands the pain that I am going through. I try to stay strong but I'm losing faith. I want to live with my mother in the Philippines, but life there would be difficult. Being a single parent, she might not be able to provide us with an education. I might not have the opportunity to get a good job so I can provide for my own family. And I do not want to add to her problems. Then again, staying here in America means that I will have to continue being separated from my family. Even if I have better opportunities here, how good can life be if I'm not with my family? I need the chance to grow up with my family—a family that was taken away from me during my childhood. At the same time, I want to provide a better future for my family, so that they do not have to suffer the bad conditions in the Philippines, such as flood and pollution. I know that taking care of them would mean, in some cases, sacrificing my own happiness.

Right now, it's important for me to maintain my positive attitude, but I'm facing a difficult situation that's tearing me in two. This is my only chance to live, so I will do my best to enjoy life. I realize that God can take back his own creations to teach us to understand and appreciate the treasures we have in our lives. I can no longer see my father, but his soul, along with all of the memories I have of him, remains in my heart.

Attempts to Revive Filipinotown, Los Angeles

Wendy Lee

*About 700,000 Filipino Americans live in Los Angeles County,
which has the largest Filipino population of any county in the
United States. However, as Wendy Lee describes in this selection,
Filipino Americans have not created a tight knit ethnic enclave
in Los Angeles—in part because even new arrivals from the
Philippines speak English well. Nonetheless, some Filipino Americans have succeeded in having a 2.1-square-mile area on the
edge of the city of Los Angeles designated as "Historic Filipinotown." Lee describes the efforts of Filipino Americans to create a
sense of pride in part of a town that has historic roots in the
Filipino community but notes that progress has been slow. Wendy
Lee is a staff writer for the* Los Angeles Times.

Signs at the edge of downtown mark the cultural home of
Los Angeles' largest Asian group. But little else of their
presence is apparent.

Historic Filipinotown won the designation three years ago
[2002] after a decades-long battle, with hopes that the blue
sign would lead to the rebirth of the community. But Filipinos
living in scattered locales, including West Covina and Carson,
have found little reason to drive into the working-class neighborhood of car repair shops and mini-marts.

Once a cultural nexus bustling with community events,
the 2.1-square-mile area is now host to weed-filled lots and
defaced storefronts with locked gates and barred windows.

A lone trumpet plays a few bars from the song of the
Mexican Hat Dance, breaking the neighborhood's short-lived

Wendy Lee, "Filipinotown Searching for Its Center; Leaders Are Trying to Lure Filipino
Americans Back to a Historic Neighborhood by Building a Sense of Community," *Los
Angeles Times*, September 13, 2005, p. B3. Copyright © 2005 *Los Angeles Times*. All
rights reserved. Reproduced by permission.

silence on a Sunday afternoon, only to be drowned out by roaring buses billowing clouds of exhaust. Elderly Filipinos lug grocery bags as they walk slowly across the uneven pavement, passing small stores with signs in Spanish, Chinese and Korean. It's easy to miss what's Filipino in the area.

Little Filipino About Filipinotown

Historic Filipinotown, some business owners and residents say, remains mired in the same problems that have been plaguing it for the last decade: declining economic activity and dwindling community unity. Perhaps most significant, it remains as nearly invisible to the outside community as it ever was. Filipinos make up less than 15% of the area's 40,000 residents, according to the district's 2002 study; 65% are Latino.

"It will always be historic until Filipinos begin to flex their muscles and work together and actually develop the area," said Joseph Bernardo, field deputy for Councilman Eric Garcetti, whose district covers Historic Filipinotown. Without direct community action, Bernardo said, "it will always remain a historic tribute. It won't become like a vibrant ethnic enclave like a Chinatown or Koreatown."

Still, community leaders and activists said they are slowly buying vacant properties so that Filipino Americans can reclaim and develop the community. They plan to build affordable housing, mostly for seniors, and to offer more cultural activities including spoken word and musical performances to lure Filipinos living in Southern California.

The largest concentration of Filipino Americans in Greater Los Angeles is in Carson, where they account for 18% of the population, according to the 2000 Census. The city of Los Angeles has the most Filipino Americans, 101,062 in 2000, with concentrations in Eagle Rock and Studio City. Other centers include Cerritos, where Filipinos make up 12% of the population; West Covina, 9%; Buena Park, 6%; and Long Beach, 4%.

Filipinos Prefer Suburbs

But rather than shopping in Historic Filipinotown, Filipino Americans in the San Gabriel Valley and other areas say they prefer to go to suburban malls in West Covina that have large Filipino-owned supermarkets and restaurants.

Michelle Nadala, who works at Manila Gifts in an open-air mall in West Covina, waved her arm toward the stores brimming with religious items, Filipino music and seashell decorations. "This is the best place to call Filipinotown," she said.

Some Filipino Americans, including 23-year-old Patrick Manabat of Roland Heights, weren't aware Historic Filipinotown exists. Manabat is used to getting his Filipino meals, like noodle dish pancit and spicy beef dish kari-kari, in West Covina, at one of South Azusa Avenue's plazas.

"Instead of going there [Historic Filipinotown], I go someplace else," he said.

Battle for a Name

Reversing the lack of interest was the goal of community leaders, who won the official Filipinotown designation three years ago after a 20-year battle for Filipinos to be recognized as a community and for their historical contributions to Los Angeles.

Unlike other Asian immigrant groups, Filipino Americans did not gather in large numbers in ethnic enclaves like Chinatown or Koreatown because they already spoke English well. In the Philippines, colonized by the United States in 1898, English is taught in schools along with Tagalog, the country's official language.

Filipino Americans have been living in Historic Filipinotown since the 1920s, when the Filipino Christian Church was built on North Union Avenue, said Teresita Dery, librarian at the Filipino American Library, a nonprofit organization seeking to preserve cultural heritage.

In the 1980s, community organizations began to push for signs to designate the area as Filipino, but there were disagreements among disparate groups on the area's size or name, said Joel Jacinto, executive director of Search to Involve Filipino Americans, a nonprofit group dedicated to the area's economic development and to providing community health services and programs.

Jacinto said Garcetti, who was running against Mike Woo for the 13th District City Council seat in 2001, approached the groups and asked what they wanted. Their primary request was for the historic designation, which Garcetti included in his platform. He also pledged to hire Filipinos as staffers and push for justice for Filipino World War II veterans. In return for those promises, Filipino Americans voted in significant numbers for Garcetti, Jacinto said.

Garcetti won the election, and a year later the blue signs went up, marking the area bounded by the Hollywood Freeway on the north, Beverly Boulevard on the south, Hoover Street on the west and Glendale Boulevard on the east.

Deterioration and Apathy

But since then, some residents and business owners said efforts to revitalize the area into a cultural home have stalled. Old foam cups, sticky ice cream wrappers and spoiled food litter the streets. Historic Filipinotown's third-year designation anniversary passed in August with no official communitywide event.

"In order for Historic Filipinotown to develop, it's going to take the participation of very many different sectors of our community working together, and that in [itself] is our own greatest challenge and opportunity," Jacinto said. "[It's] definitely possible that it's out there for us, as long as we're able to work collaboratively together. That's the rub."

Part of the push targets senior citizens who live in the area and those who community leaders hope will move there.

Jacinto's group, Search to Involve Filipino Americans, has built two projects, with a total of 92 units, for low- to moderate-income families and is planning 162 more, about 80 of which will be senior housing.

Leaders also want to make the area visually distinct. A $2.1-million Historic Filipinotown Pavilion at Beverly Boulevard and Union Avenue will showcase a new pocket park next to the Filipino American Mural, the nation's largest mural focusing on the ethnic group.

For now, the mural remains locked behind a fence, its description tagged and decayed.

Plans for the Future

Filipino crosswalk designs, based on traditional weave patterns, have been placed in three intersections. Other plans include streetlight banners and purple orchid trees, familiar sights in the Philippines, Bernardo said. So far, 25 orchid trees have been planted on Temple Street, with 75 to 100 more coming in the next year or so, he added.

There are also preliminary plans from various community groups for a statue of Jose Rizal, a writer and Philippine national hero who was executed in 1896. Garcetti's office is planning a memorial in Lake Street Park for Filipino veterans of World War II, Bernardo said.

Two recently opened art spaces—Tribal Cafe and Remy's on Temple—showcasing Philippine artwork have attracted some suburban Filipinos to the area, as has a community art show in June organized by the Assn. for the Advancement of Filipino American Arts and Culture.

"It takes a long time, but someone has got to do it," said Joselyn Geaga-Rosenthal, owner of Remy's. Unlike Koreatown, Historic Filipinotown does not have streets that allow for a good mixture of businesses to prosper, said Ken Klein, head of USC's East Asian Library. The main corridors of Historic Filipinotown, including Beverly Boulevard, have "lots of small businesses that Filipinos could develop, little grocery stores, fast food places. . . . But there's no real center and no real opportunity for major kinds of investments," Klein said.

But Filipino American community activists are still optimistic. Already the designation has given Filipino Americans more political bite, as Mayor Antonio Villaraigosa visited the area during his campaign.

"We don't want to be known as the longest community sign in the city of Los Angeles," said James Santa Maria, a Filipino community activist. "We want it to mean something, and we want to make sure it endures."

Filipinos Today

Rick Bonus

In this selection historian Rick Bonus describes life for Filipino Americans, analyzing their economic status, workplace discrimination, and their attempts to assimilate into American culture. According to Bonus, Filipino Americans are perceived as economically successful, but studies reveal that of all Asian Americans, Filipinos' per capita income is lower. However, most Filipinos do graduate from high school and become professionals or managers. Bonus writes that although the blatant racism Filipino Americans faced in the past is no longer rampant, many believe that they still face more subtle forms of discrimination in the workplace, especially in terms of job promotion. Many Filipino Americans have sought to succeed in American society by assimilating and sometimes abandoning their cultural heritage; however, Bonus observes, quite a few Filipino Americans do meet regularly in churches, community halls, and other places to socialize or conduct political organization.

Rick Bonus is a Filipino American and professor of American Ethnic Studies at the University of Washington, Seattle. He is also the editor of Contemporary Asian American Communities: Intersections and Divergences *with Linda Trinh Võ.*

Facing a different set of conditions and circumstances than those experienced by the previous generation, many [Filipino Americans] have been involved in issue-oriented causes such as voter registration, affirmative action, bilingual education, workplace discrimination, and citizenship entitlements. Along with other Asian Americans, Filipino Americans confront civil rights issues that involve hate crimes, access to police protection, educational opportunity, employment dis-

Rick Bonus, "Filipinos and Filipinas in America," in *Locating Filipino Americans: Ethnicity, and the Cultural Politics of Space*. Philadelphia: Temple University Press, 2000, pp. 52–55. Copyright © 2000 by Temple University. All rights reserved. Used by permission of Temple University Press.

crimination, health care, media representation, violence against women, and religious freedom, among others. The most common perception among Filipino Americans I talked to is that more covert forms of racism exist particularly in job promotion and the curtailment of language rights in the workplace, and in access to higher-level educational opportunities.

Economic Participation

The economic participation of Filipinos after 1965, however, is another story. According to the 1990 census, Filipinos are more likely than the population as a whole to participate in the labor force. They have the highest labor participation rate among all Asian Americans (75.4 percent of Filipinos sixteen years old and over) and the most families with three or more workers (29.6 percent) compared with other Asian Americans. Most Filipinos are high school graduates or possess higher degrees (82.6 percent; third after Japanese and Asian Indian Americans) and are managers or professionals; in technical, sales, and administrative support; and in service. But these figures may not entirely coincide with their perceived "economic success." Five percent of the Filipino American labor force is unemployed (close to the 6.3 percent unemployed figure for all Americans), and 6.4 percent is considered poor. And even if many are in occupations that are deemed higher paying, Filipinos' average per capita income was only $13,616—lower than that of all Asian Americans ($13,806). These figures suggest the diversity of the Filipino American population and, possibly, the underemployment of its professional pool.

The extent to which the Filipino American population today is principally a labor force and marginally a political force is testament to the continued dependence of the United States on a racially stratified and gendered labor pool that is at once treated and perceived as, or desired to be, silent and docile. Filipinos occupy peculiar niches in the U.S. terrain. Encouraged to immigrate as vital and integral components of the nation's economy, they are simultaneously marked and placed as outsiders, alien, or foreign to such an extent that their historical presence in the educational, political, and social realms is marginalized or even erased.

Responses to Racism

Because of or despite these conditions, many Filipino third wavers try to ignore or brush aside the impact of racism on their lives by living apart from mainstream society and working long hours or taking extra jobs to gain greater financial security. Many also try to "pass" by "acting like an American," as several respondents have said, paying the price of forsaking their native culture. A number of them, for instance, have chosen to speak to their children in English exclusively to protect them from possibly being maltreated in school and other public places. The common perception is that they run the risk of being "punished" if they continue to act like the Filipinos that they are. "This race thing is new to us," said one interviewee. "We never learn this from the TV shows we saw back home. But we know how to survive. We know how to make it. We'll even exceed what they can do."

To many of those I talked to, there is a dark side to assimilation. Even the formal conferment of citizenship by way of naturalization and a U.S. passport does not guarantee full acceptance into society. To them, these can indeed be giant strides in terms of being able to vote and have a voice in how the nation is run. But they know that these are also but small (though significant) steps on the long road to visibility and recognition.

Modern Communities

In the meantime, a good number of Filipinos today have found refuge in places where they can be among and enjoy the company of people who are like them and therefore are likely to treat them in more positive ways. Many of them are beginning to realize that their common experiences of racism and invisibility have roots that span generations of contact between their former colonizers and their nation of origin or descent. In places where they see other Filipinos, the stories that they exchange with each other often reflect this shared historical and contemporary experience.

These places include churches, commercial centers, and community halls, which become venues for Filipino American gatherings, meetings, and regular interaction. Filipino American social and political organizations, some of which were started by first- and second-wave immigrants decades ago, continue to flourish and thrive in support of local needs and interests. Commercial establishments like stores, restaurants, beauty and barber shops, and video rental stores dot a number of neighborhoods to cater to Filipinos' demands. Community newspapers, as well as statewide and nationwide magazines, link disparate population groups and provide spaces for conversing with each other on matters affecting their interconnected lives. These are the kinds of spaces that have bridged a diverse and heterogeneous population, across generations and subgroups, against shared experiences of racism.

Diversity Within Filipino American Communities

Filipino American settlements today are multiple, scattered, diverse, and heterogeneous. To refer to a Filipino American community, one must include men and women who came to the United States at different times; who were born in the United States and who were born in the Philippines; who are unskilled, semiskilled, and professional; who are and are not educated; who came from and live in urban and rural areas; who came in as parents and as children; and who are offspring of both early and recent arrivals. In other words, the breadth and variety of Filipino immigration to the United States necessitates the signification of a Filipino American community in the plural.

Such a plurality is evident in the Southern California Filipino American communities I have studied. Both the Los Angeles and San Diego Filipino population groups are predominantly third wavers as opposed to oldtimers (as first and second wavers are locally called). There is also substantial representation of parents of professionals who are retired or working menial jobs, of second- and third-generation offspring of earlier immigrants, and of skilled workers in the military (primarily in San Diego, since its naval stations and their outlying environs have been home to many recruits). Parts of the counties have also preserved in varying degrees the communities of earlier immigrants. . . . The 1990 census counts 219,653 Filipino Americans in the county of Los Angeles and 95,945 in San Diego County. They have settled in a variety of neighborhoods, depending significantly on their class status.

CHAPTER 4

COMING TO
AMERICA

Accomplished
Filipino Americans

Jessica Hagedorn: Writer

Jessica Hagedorn, as interviewed by Kay Bonetti

Filipino American writer Jessica Tarahata Hagedorn was born in Manila, Philippines, in 1949. She was raised in the Philippines until the age of fourteen, when she moved to San Francisco, California. She studied theater and music at American Conservatory Theater, and eventually moved to New York in 1978. Although her ancestry includes Scotch, Irish, Spanish, and French roots, it is her Filipino heritage with which she identifies the most strongly. In 1990 she published Dogeaters, *a novel that received the National Book Award and was later adapted into a stage play. Hagedorn is also a poet, musician, and editor. In this interview with Kay Bonetti, Hagedorn describes how her identity as a Filipina American has shaped her literary work.*

Kay Bonetti is the founder of the American Audio Prose Library.

*I*nterviewer *(Kay Bonetti): What is your particular ethnic background? I would like to talk about that a little bit because the whole question of what it is to be Filipino runs throughout your work.*

Hagedorn: I'm part Spanish. My paternal grandfather came from Spain via Singapore to Manila. On my mother's side it's more mixture, with a Filipino mother and a father who was Scotch Irish-French; you know, white American hybrid. And I also have on my father's side a great-great-grandmother who was Chinese. So, I'm a hybrid.

Interviewer: Assuming that it is you talking in one of your prose pieces from Danger and Beauty, *you've actualy described your-*

Jessica Hagedorn, as interviewed by Kay Bonetti, "An Interview with Jessica Hagedorn," *The Missouri Review*, vol. XVIII, no. 1, 1995, www.missourireview.com. Copyright © 1994 American Audio Prose Library, Inc. Reproduced by permission.

self this way: *"I was born in the Philippines. I am a quintessential bastard. My roots are dubious." Where does the bastard part come from?*

Hagedorn: Well, there's always a bastard in the family isn't there? And certainly with the Spaniards, they left a lot of bastards around. I'm an underdog person, so I align myself with those who seem to be not considered valuable in polite society. I think for a lot of so-called post-colonial peoples, there's a feeling of not being quite legitimate, of not being pure enough. And to me that's the beauty and strength of the culture—that it is mixed.

Filipino Cultures

Interviewer: Can you tell us a little bit about the basic mix of cultures. In Dogeaters, *you refer in one section to eighty dialects and languages spoken.*

Hagedorn: There are many, many tribes who speak their own dialect but who have no say in what's going on in government, for example. So we have to think about that too. But people speak Tagalog, which is also known as "Pilipino" now—the nationalists claim it's Pilipino. Many speak English, and some of the older generation still speak a very fluent Spanish, because that was part of the culture at one time, or a mixture of the three. For example, in my household sometimes a sentence could have all three languages in it at once. It's not like sometimes we spoke the whole sentence in English and other times in Tagalog. No, it was all in the language. Like a "Tag-lish" or something. And there are many, many more languages. When the Spanish came over to do their colonizing, these islands with disparate tribes suddenly got lumped together. And not everybody necessarily got along. There was, according to some Filipino historians, a matriarchal society which was wiped out. Animism was practiced. Some of the people are highlanders; some are lowland peoples; some are Muslims because at some point in our history the Arab traders had come through there, so there is a very powerful Muslim faction in the southern region of the Philippines.

Interviewer: With all the backgrounds that you've said are prominent in your family, why is it that you identify yourself with the Asian experience?

Hagedorn: Because that's been my experience.

Interviewer: Even though your father was Spanish?

Hagedorn: Yes, but he was Filipino Spanish. There's a difference. When mestizos go to Spain, they are looked down upon. "Ah, you live in the Philippines." You know, it's a class thing, even if you're rich. There's always this motherland-fatherland bit, and then there's the colonies. My identity is linked to my grandmother, who's pure Filipino, as pure as you can probably get. And that shaped my imagination. So that's how I identify. I also identify as a Latin person, a person who has Latin blood. Certainly, I'm exploring that now. And I've lived now in North America close to thirty years. In terms of my politics, I feel a political alliance too, with the Asian community here. . . .

Interviewer: You've described the "memory of Manila" as "the central character of the novel I am writing." How much of the Philippines of Dogeaters, *because you left at the age of fourteen, is the product of memory, as you've implied, and how much is the product of augmented memory and research?*

Hagedorn: It's both. I think it's very important that it's memory first because too much research and factual writing can kill a book. I wasn't trying to write the absolute "real deal" story of the Philippines. I was only writing about a certain time frame and also about a certain group of people in a city, you know. This is not the quintessential Philippines novel.

I mean, I don't know who's going to write that. There are many writers there who have grappled with creating the epic Philippine novel.

Interviewer: "I am the other, the exile within," you have also said. Do you think that in some cases, or in your case, it was an advantage to be an outsider as it were, writing from memory, in order to deal with such a large subject?

Hagedorn: Having distance always helps. It gives you a certain overview that when you are right up against it, it's very difficult to make certain choices.

Interviewer: How did you come to the characters that surely were not a part of your growing up in Manila at all, such as Joey?

Hagedorn: But they were. I mean I didn't go to those bars when I was eight years old, but those people were always there. That's why the book jumps back and forth in time. When I was old enough and going back to the Philippines more often, it was the time of martial law when it was very repressive on the surface. At the same time there was a lot of corruption, and pornography was part of life even though you had this regime that was trying to present itself as being squeaky clean. Well, it was the height of the worst moral decay. I was on my own then, so I could explore what I wanted to explore. And I already had the idea that one day I was going to write this novel, so I made myself open to a lot of different experiences and met all kinds of people. I wanted to get to that underbelly because I felt like those were the people who nobody cared about and nobody thought about and they were too easily dismissed. . . .

Confronting Demons

Interviewer: You've written that at one point you scorned yourself and that it was only later, after you had left the Philippines "to settle in the country of my oppressor"—which you have also

said you never thought of as being the oppressor back then—
"that I learned to confront my demons and reinvent my own
history." First, what are the demons you're talking about con-
fronting?

Hagedorn: The demons of identity are certainly some of the
demons I confront. God, I don't have to list all my demons,
do I Kay? But in that particular sentence I meant this sort of
condition of who am I? I am of mixed blood. Where are my
allegiances? Is there an easy answer? No there isn't. I wanted
to have clarity about what I was doing. Who am I as an artist,
as a woman? Now whether or not I choose to answer those
questions, I still get disturbed by them. Those themes perme-
ate my work, so that's part of the demonology of my life. And
I think about issues of mortality and immortality. I'm starting
to confront now living in the United States as opposed to living back in the Philippines. Why I've decided to do that. It's
important to me to know why, and would I die here? That's
my new question. Is this the country where I want to die and
be buried? If so, maybe it's because this is a country that allows you to reinvent yourself. . . .

Immigration to San Francisco

Interviewer: At the age of fourteen, you were taken by your
mother from Manila out of one very multi-ethnic culture into
America, another multi-ethnic culture. What was that like?

Hagedorn: It was terrible at first. Luckily, she chose to live in
San Francisco and not in someplace where we would've stood
out. There was a multi-ethnic community and, luckily, there
was Chinatown, for God's sake, which we constantly went to.
It was the closest thing to Manila we could find. I was at such
a terrible age, so gawky and awkward, and I didn't know
whether I was grown up or still a child. So it was a weird
time. Also exciting. I mean I had always fancied that I would
travel once I was old enough, and live in many places in the

133

world, so I had that adventurer thing anyway. It's just that it happened a little too abruptly. And I was uprooted in the middle of my school work and I wasn't ready to go then, it was not the time. Too many adjustments too fast. But I was also flexible and we all were tougher than we thought. It took a turn for the better when I realized that one of the positive things about it was that as a female person, I suddenly had a sense of freedom that I never had growing up in Manila in that over-protected colonial environment—the girl with her chaperones and everything that still goes on, that kind of tradition. And even though girls are not discouraged from going to school, they're still expected to marry and have a family and that's the subtext of everything. In America, suddenly I was free from those shackles. And because my mother was preoccupied with trying to make a new life for herself, reinventing herself at age forty, she could not control me as much as she would have liked too. So there was a pay off for me.

Interviewer: Was this when you started writing?

Hagedorn: I started writing seriously then. I had always written. As a child, I loved to read and I always thought of myself as a writer. You know, I was very dramatic. I would write little poems and I loved to make little comic books. I would illustrate them, four-page comic books, and thought of myself as a writer. When I was fourteen, my mother gave me a typewriter, thank heavens, and I guess she thought that would be a healthy way to keep me at home. I would type poems and read. . . .

Interviewer: Is there any sense in which you are writing for a purpose, to correct stereotypes or to reinvent history in a way that corrects wrongs?

Hagedorn: If I were to write with that agenda in mind, then I'd destroy the writing. No, I write really because I have to and if the writing also destroys some of those myths and subverts forms and makes people question the very idea of the writer, the woman, the Filipino-American, the whatever, great!

Antonio Taguba:
U.S. Army General

Bert Eljera

Antonio Taguba is the second Filipino American military officer ever to rise to the rank of general. Taguba was born October 31, 1950, in Manila, Philippines. His family moved to Hawaii when he was eleven, and he graduated from Idaho State University in 1972. He is currently Deputy Commanding General for Support, Third U.S. Army, U.S. Armed Forces Central Command in Kuwait. Taguba holds three master's degrees, and is the recipient of the Distinguished Service Medal for meritorious service. In 2004, he became well known as the author of a classified report about cases of torture at the Abu Ghraib prison in Iraq. In this profile of Taguba, Asian Week *journalist Bert Eljera describes how Taguba's experience as a Filipino American immigrant have influenced his military career. Taguba states that while he believes it's important to preserve the many valuable aspects of his Filipino culture, he also is proud that Filipinos have integrated so successfully into American society.*

Bert Eljera is a freelance writer and former staff writer for the Los Angeles Times.

> *"Hawaii opened my mind to the capabilities and opportunities in America. The diversity gave me a wide range to seek opportunities and to relate to other people."*—Antonio Taguba

While the U.S. Armed Forces are often held up as models for racial integration in this country, that cannot be said of its officer corps, particularly among its generals and

Bert Eljera, "Military Officer: Army Appoints Its Second Fil-Am General," *Asian Week*, August 1–7, 1997. © 1998 *Asian Week*. Reproduced by permission.

senior officers. Like the board rooms of most private corporations, generals of the major services predominantly are white males—although blacks have made some headway, most notably in the person of Gen. Colin Powell, the former head of the Joint Chiefs of Staff.

Asian Pacific Americans, however, are at the bottom of the totem pole in the military ranks. There is no APA flag officer on active duty in the U.S. Navy or general in the U.S. Air Force; the same is true for the U.S. Marines.

But, the U.S. Army seems to be a more hospitable ground for APAs. A lieutenant general and a brigadier general are actively serving, and a third general is going through the confirmation process and is likely to get his star in the next few weeks.

If confirmed by the U.S. Senate, Col. Antonio Taguba will become the second Filipino American general in the U.S. Army[1], joining Brig. Gen. Edward Soriano, who is the director of Operations, Readiness, and Mobilization at the Office of the Deputy Chief of Staff for Operations and Plans at the Pentagon.

"I'm very humbled by this recognition," said Taguba, reached at his new post at the Army Force Camp at Fort McPherson in Atlanta. "There are a lot of people to thank for my success—fellow soldiers, friends, my family, and my kids who have withstood the triumphs and tribulations of life in the military."

Taguba is temporarily assigned as special assistant to the camp's commanding general, Gen. David Bramlett, and does not yet know what unit he will command.

Before his promotion, he was the commander of the 2nd Brigade, 4th Infantry Division, at Fort Hood, Texas. His military career spans 25 years and includes a three-year stint in Germany and six years in Korea.

1. Taguba was confirmed by the Senate.

Family Life

It's a long way from Sampaloc, Manila, where Taguba was born on Oct. 31, 1950, to a large, deeply religious family. His father, Tomas, is a retired Army sergeant. His mother, Maria, stayed home to raise him, two other brothers, and five sisters.

"I had an absentee father who was in the Army, but I had an enjoyable childhood," said Taguba, who still remembers watching television on a black-and-white set, attending fiestas, and visiting relatives in Cagayan, a province north of Manila.

While he was attracted to the military at an early age because his father was in the Army, he said it was his mother and grandmother who raised him who had the most influence in his life.

"It's part of our culture to respect elders, give thanks to the Lord, to be forgiving, and be supportive of your family. I've learned those early in life," Taguba said.

Ethnicity and Success

When he was 11 years old, his family moved to Hawaii, where he graduated from Leilehua High School in 1968. He said he benefited from the diversity and openness of the people in Hawaii and felt that his ethnicity was no hindrance to success.

"[Hawaii] opened my mind to the capabilities and opportunities in America," Taguba said. "The diversity gave me a wide range to seek opportunities and to relate to other people. I had friends from all races. I tend to like it that way. It has helped me in my career."

Seeking a little adventure, Taguba left Hawaii and enrolled at Idaho State University, where he graduated in 1972. He joined the U.S. Army shortly thereafter. He steadily rose through the ranks, graduating from prestigious military-training schools, including the U.S. Army Command and General Staff College, College of Naval Command and Staff, and the U.S. Army War College.

He also holds master's degrees in public administration from Webster University, in international relations from Salve Regina College, and in national security and strategic studies from the U.S. Naval War College.

Taguba commanded a tank company of a mechanized infantry division in Germany, and was a battalion commander and later executive officer of the combined Republic of Korea-U.S. Forces in Korea.

From June 1995 to June of this year, he was commander of the 2nd Brigade, 4th Infantry Division, at Fort Hood. For his services, he has received various decorations, including the Meritorious Service Medal (Five Oak Leaf Clusters), Army Commendation Medal (Two Oak Leaf Clusters), the Army Achievement Medal (One Oak Leaf Cluster) and the Army General Staff identification badge.

Preserving Filipino Culture

"I take it with great pride that we are able to assimilate ourselves into the American society," Taguba said. "We have shown we can contribute to society, at the same time preserve our Filipino American heritage and culture."

Taguba lives in Peachtree City, Ga., with his wife, Debbie, and children, Lindsay, 15, and Sean, 12.

Larry Dulay Itliong: Activist

Stephen Magagnini

In the following profile journalist Stephen Magagnini describes the accomplishments of pioneering Filipino American labor leader Larry Dulay Itliong. Itliong was born in Pangasinan, Philippines, on October 25, 1913. At the age of sixteen he boarded a vessel bound for Seattle, Washington, with other Filipinos in search of work in the United States. Itliong, who spoke nine Philippine dialects, was appalled by the exploitive labor conditions he found in both Alaskan canneries and the agricultural fields of the West Coast. In 1930 he joined striking Filipino lettuce pickers in Seattle and began to take an active role in the organization of farmworkers and unions. A founder (Cesar Chavez, Dolores Huerta, and Philip Vera Cruz) of the United Farm Workers Organizing Committee (UFWOC), Itliong successfully fought for improvements in the living conditions of farmworkers and laborers. Itliong died on February 8, 1977. On April 6, 2006, he was recognized with a California Assembly resolution for his contributions to the California labor movement.

Stephen Magagnini is a senior writer for the Sacramento Bee *and a journalism fellow at Stanford University. He is also a recipient of the Columbia Graduate School of Journalism Lifetime Achievement Award.*

He lies buried in an ordinary grave amid the vineyards and almond orchards of the Central Valley, where he and his fellow farm workers toiled for decades in the broiling sun without toilets or cold water. Few know that Larry Dulay Itliong, a Filipino immigrant of extraordinary courage, transformed California and the nation when he triggered the Delano table grape growers' strike of 1965.

Stephen Magagnini, "New Light Shed on Pioneering Filipino American," *The Sacramento Bee*, December 28, 1996, p. A1. Reproduced by permission.

Itliong—who had been organizing immigrant farm workers and cannery workers for over 30 years—led a walkout of 1,500 Filipino grape-pickers on Sept. 8, 1965, to protest low wages and miserable working conditions.

Twelve days later, his striking manongs (Filipino "brothers") were joined by Cesar Chavez and his National Farm Workers Association. The two groups formed the United Farm Workers, which waged one of the most famous strikes in American history—the five-year boycott of Central Valley table-grape growers.

The boycott inspired the student strikes of the late 1960s at San Francisco State, UC Berkeley and elsewhere that resulted in the first ethnic studies departments.

Now, 20 years after his death, Itliong's never-before-published papers and interviews with friends and relatives reveal a charismatic, stogie-smoking visionary who organized workers from Alaska to Chile and captured the imagination of a generation of '60s activists. "While speaking for the pinoys (Filipino men)," he would write, the bosses "are always trying to buy me off or the government is trying to deport me." But with organization came power, and with power came respect.

"He was my hero," said prominent Filipino American historian Fred Cordova, who wants Itliong given his proper place in history.

"He awakened our Filipino American consciousness and the responsibilities that went with it," said Cordova. "It wasn't so much a matter of being proud of who you were, but what are you going to do about it to improve this country?"

After a xenophobic America shut its doors to nearly all immigrants in 1924, Itliong was among the 50,000 Filipinos recruited by farmers in California and Hawaii in need of cheap labor.

The son of a rice farmer and sari maker, Itliong left Pangasinan province in the Philippines at 16 with a sixth-grade education and dreams of becoming a lawyer and politician.

He had read that America was a place where "you pick money on trees and also the land of justice." Except, he said, "the only justice given to us we hassle for."

He wrote about the packed ship bound for Seattle on which he and other ambitious young Filipinos had "no fresh air to breathe. . . . The ship smells so bad most everybody got sick. As a matter of fact, a few died."

He arrived in 1929, having never slept in a bed or used a toilet. A year later, he joined striking lettuce pickers in Washington.

Itliong learned the American way by listening to trials and other court proceedings. "That's how he got his knowledge," said his sixth and last wife, Nellie. "One time he heard an organization was going to have a hearing in another town. He didn't have a way of going there, so he hid in the back of a train. When he jumped off, somehow his right hand got caught and he lost three fingers—he only had a thumb and forefinger left."

Ray Paular, a Sacramento pinoy who worked with Itliong from Delano to Ketchikan, said Itliong lost his fingers while working as a butcher in an Alaskan cannery. "They used to take the fish, and shove it into a machine one by one," Paular said. "You do that hour after hour and you're in danger of losing your coordination."

Paular, who spent nine summers in Alaska, said Itliong helped establish the Alaska Cannery Workers Union in the 1930s.

"There must have been at least 1,500 Filipino cannery workers," he said. "When I was 16, I said I would never come back to this place. I was working like a dog. When the fish came in, you worked two, three days around the clock. We had different bunkhouses and menus than white workers—we were (like) indentured workers."

Itliong ran for union office under the slogan "militant—frank—capable," and helped get a contract that called for eight-hour days plus overtime, Paular said.

Like thousands of other migrants, he laid railroad track, harvested sugar beets in Montana and South Dakota, worked in canneries from San Pedro to Alaska, and picked produce from Canada to the Mexican border. Whenever Filipinos had a problem, the 5-foot 5-inch organizer, cigar in hand, spoke up for them.

Itliong served as vice president of the cannery workers union in Seattle in 1953 and still found time to help orchestrate an asparagus strike in Stockton.

In 1956, he formed the Filipino Farm Labor Union.

Itliong was briefly married to a woman he met at the New Continent Pool Hall in Stockton's "Little Manila," home to 20,000 Filipinos. He then married a woman who left him after their third child was born. In 1968, he had another failed marriage to a woman he met in Manila.

Never one to shy away from matrimony, in 1969 he wed Nellie, a Latina farm worker with three children. They had one child, bringing the number of kids in Itliong's modest Delano tract home to seven.

In 1965, Itliong and Pete Velasco led a Filipino strike of Coachella Valley grape growers that resulted in higher pay.

Emboldened by the success of the Coachella strike, they decided to strike in Delano, where most table grapes are grown.

Most Filipino workers were in their 60s. Itliong spoke nine Filipino dialects, giving "them a lot of courage," said his widow. "He would say, 'Let's go, don't be scared, I will be in the front—just follow me.'"

Chavez, who had been carefully building his own farm workers' organization farm by farm for three years, was not ready to strike.

"Our worry was the Filipinos would abandon the strike," said UFW co-founder Dolores Huerta. "Some of them were beaten up by the growers (who) would shut off the gas and the lights and the water in the labor camps."

The growers' brutality forced Chavez's hand, Huerta said, and within two weeks, 1,200 Latino farm workers joined the strike.

"For 80 years prior to 1965, every organizing attempt had been defeated, every strike had been crushed, the only law they knew was the law of the jungle and abuse and contempt and violence against farm workers was commonplace," said Marc Grossman, Chavez's longtime spokesman.

"Larry and Cesar's great contribution was they crossed racial barriers," Grossman said. Growers had historically pitted one race against another, he said, hiring Latinos to break Filipino strikes and vice-versa.

The alliance angered some workers on each side. "The Filipino community was very upset with Itliong because he joined with Chavez," said Jack Pandol, dean of Delano grape growers.

Pandol denied growers beat Filipino strikers, and accused Itliong of using young toughs to intimidate the manongs into striking.

"One day I went to take pictures of him in front of a packing house, and he grabbed my camera and broke it," said Pandol. Itliong was arrested for breaking the camera and spent the night in jail.

In December 1965, United Auto Workers President Walter Reuther called for a national boycott against Delano grape products and gave the strikers $5,000 a month. Clergy backed the boycott, and a Harris poll showed that 17 million people stopped buying table grapes.

Itliong let his hair grow long and spoke passionately from coast to coast to raise money for the strikers. His words galvanized students who struck at San Francisco State and UC Berkeley.

"The ethnic studies departments you see now are the result of those strikes," said James Sobredo, a Filipino-American instructor at Berkeley.

In July 1970, the Delano strike finally ended. "We got wage increases, a medical plan for farm workers, we set up five clinics, a day care center and a school," Huerta said.

In the process, the UFW did away with the system of crew leaders, which had served Filipinos well for a half century.

Latinos outnumbered Filipinos in the UFW, and in 1971 Itliong—his power diminished—resigned as second-in-command after questions were raised about the $550 a month he received to support his wife and seven kids.

He criticized the "intellectuals" who had surrounded Chavez, saying they did "not relate to the thinking of the farm workers." He wrote, "My lone voice in the policy making is but a feeble voice."

After leaving the UFW, he went to Brazil and Chile to organize farm workers. Though weakened by multiple sclerosis in his last years, Itliong never stopped fighting for the rights of retired manongs, many of whom had worked the fields for half a century.

"When a worker grows old, weak and cannot any longer be used by the growers, he is told he can no longer stay in the camps. . . . It does not matter that he has no savings, very little income, no relatives who can house him," Itliong wrote to then-Sen. Walter Mondale in 1973.

"As bad as the conditions were for him in the camps, it is much worse for him on his own. These old and forgotten Filipino farm workers, cast off like old shoes after having given the most productive years of their lives doing thankless but vital work—feeding the nation—(are) forced to spend their waning years in dilapidated, rat-infested hotels."

Itliong founded the Filipino American Political Association and oversaw the creation of Agbayani Village, a center for retired Filipino farm workers in Delano.

He helped aging Filipinos find jobs, do their taxes, and collect Social Security, said his widow.

After Itliong's death on Feb. 8, 1977, at age 63, Chavez praised him as "a true pioneer in the farm workers movement."

Today, his family is fractured. His oldest son, Larry Jr., disappeared on the streets of Los Angeles and hasn't been heard from for five years, said another son, Johnny. Of the 40 manongs who once occupied Agbayani Village, only two remain.

"I'd like to see his grave site included as a national shrine, and that the name Larry Itliong is mentioned in the same breath as Cesar Chavez in ethnic studies courses," Cordova said. "His impact on the Filipino American experience is unsurpassed."

Cristeta Comerford: Executive Chef

Jose Antonio Vargas

Filipino American chef Cristeta Pasia Comerford was born in Manila, Philippines, in 1962. At 23, after studying food technology at the University of the Philippines, Diliman, Comerford immigrated with her family to Chicago, Illinois. She worked as a hotel chef in Chicago before moving to Washington, DC, and traveling to study culinary arts in Austria. Her focus and culinary ability impressed many in her profession, and in 1995 she was recruited to work in the White House for President Bill Clinton. On August 14, 2005, she became the first woman and the first Filipino American to hold the title of White House Executive Chef.

In this selection Jose Antonio Vargas reports on the reaction of Comerford's family and of many in the Filipino American community to her successes. Vargas, a reporter for the Washington Post, *has written for the* Philadelphia Daily News, *the* Seattle Times, *and the* San Francisco Chronicle.

She's come a long, long, long way, this former hotel "salad girl." Before she was hired as an assistant chef in the White House in 1995, before first lady Laura Bush promoted her to White House executive chef last week [2006], Cristeta Comerford—"Cris" to her neighbors and co-workers here in the Washington area, "Teta" to her large but tight-knit Filipino family in the Chicago suburb of Morton Grove—was in charge of a salad bar.

"That's what I called her, 'salad girl.' She prepared Caesar salad, Cobb salad," says Juanito Pasia, Cristeta's older brother, trying not to laugh. It was Juanito who drove Teta—then 23,

Jose Antonio Vargas, "Hail to the Chef," *The Washington Post*, August 22, 2005, p. C1. Copyright © 2005 The Washington Post Company. Reprinted with permission.

newly arrived from the Philippines—in his blue Ford van to and from work at a Sheraton Hotel near Chicago's O'Hare International Airport. "Can you believe it?" he asks, giving another hearty laugh. "Can you believe this is happening?"

Ask the people who have worked alongside the 42-year-old Comerford around the world, whether in Chicago, Vienna or Washington, and the answer seems to be a definitive yes. Her new position as the White House's top toque—a uniquely high-profile and sought-after celebrity chef job—is an affirmation, her former bosses and co-workers say, of the hard work, focus, imperturbable demeanor and culinary talent she has shown in the kitchen.

American Success Story

"Over and over and over again," says Walter Scheib III, who as the former executive chef—hired by Hillary Rodham Clinton in 1994, then asked to resign by Laura Bush earlier this year— lured Comerford to join the White House kitchen staff in 1995. In the subsequent years, he adds, he considered her not so much his assistant chef as his "co-chef." "She's an all-around great chef, no question about it. Let me put it to you this way: In the years that I've worked with her, there's been so many dishes she's made for me, and I cannot think of anything she did that wasn't good."

Comerford, who lives in a two-story Colonial-style home in Columbia with her husband, John, and their 4-year-old daughter, Danielle, declined to be interviewed for this article. The White House is planning a "press event" in the first week of September to accommodate the hundreds of requests— "more than 500 so far and counting," says an overwhelmed Susan Whitson, Laura Bush's press secretary—to interview Comerford (who, the very moment she made headlines, left for an already-planned weeklong family vacation to Cancun, Mexico).

"White House taps 1st woman, minority as head chef," read a headline in *USA Today*.

"Her résumé reads like a classic American success story," read an editorial in the *Chicago Tribune*.

The popular comedic news program "The Daily Show" weighed in, with faux senior presidential correspondent Stephen Colbert reporting that Comerford faces a tough confirmation battle (she doesn't, of course) because she once deemed curried yams "too ethnic" (dubious, but funny).

Familial Support

Cristeta Comerford is the second youngest of 11 children, with six half brothers, one half sister and three full sisters. Everyone was everyone else's babysitter.

Born in October 1962 in Manila, she was raised in a working-class neighborhood of Sampaloc, near the sprawling campus of the University of Santo Tomas, a Catholic school founded in 1611. Honesto Pasia, her father, was an elementary school principal; Erlinda Pasia, her mother, was a dressmaker. "So driven," says Cristeta's older sister, Ofelia Aguila, a design director for the College of American Pathologists. "So ambitious."

Erlinda, who's 78 and lives with Ofelia and her family in Morton Grove, a 20-minute drive from downtown Chicago, has only one word to describe her Teta: "*Napakabait.*" That means "very kind" in Tagalog, the dominant native language in the Philippines.

"*Tuwang tuwa ang boong pamilia para sa kanya,*" says Erlinda. ("The family is very, very happy for her.")

"I could feel within my heart that joy that is kind of just overflowing," says Ofelia, recalling Teta's phone call telling her about the promotion. "Then I thought of my dad. Oh, if he were still alive!" Honesto died more than 10 years ago, before Teta started working in the White House. "He would have been very, very excited over this."

The Pasia daughters grew up in a house of food, with Erlinda as the perfectionist, hard-to-please head chef. "It's either overcooked or too salty, she would say. Too little this and too much that," says Ofelia. It was rare for the family to eat out.

Emigration from the Philippines

Filipino cuisine is determinedly eclectic, a mix of Chinese, Japanese and Spanish influence. Erlinda can whip out a classic chicken adobo, a kind of stew, or pancit canton, a kind of noodle dish, or lumpia Shanghai, the Filipino egg roll, all staples of any Filipino party, not so much "by formula," says Ofelia, but "by instinct." The mother passed that gift on to her daughters.

Encouraged by her family, Comerford studied food. She attended the University of the Philippines-Diliman, in Quezon City, and majored in food technology. Contrary to a news release issued by the White House, though, she didn't complete her degree. Juanito, an accountant and the first in the family to move to the States, had petitioned his parents, brothers and sisters to let her join him there, and Comerford opted to leave school when her visa was approved.

After stints at the Sheraton and Hyatt Regency hotels near Chicago O'Hare, Cristeta, with her husband, who's also a chef, moved here. She was a chef at two Washington restaurants—Le Grande Bistro at the Westin Hotel and the Colonnade at the former ANA Hotel. For six months, she worked as chef tournant ("revolving chef") at Le Ciel, in Vienna, Austria, sharpening her mastery of French classical techniques. Scheib, then the executive chef at the White House, recruited her.

"As a chef, you need a certain feeling, a certain way of putting food together, not just cooking it but presenting it. It's hard to describe, but she has that feeling," says Siegfried Pucher, her former boss at Le Ciel.

A Stellar Career

In her 10 years at the White House, however, her specialty has been ethnic and American cuisine. What pleased the first lady is the way Comerford can more than satisfy the president with a lunch of enchilada or cheeseburger, then turn around to cook a state dinner that pairs chilled asparagus soup and lemon cream with pan-roasted halibut and basmati rice (with pistachio nuts and currants). In fact, the dinner for 134 guests held last month in honor of Indian Prime Minister Manmohan Singh won Comerford the job.

"For those back home in the Philippines, and for the Filipinos who are working immigrants and naturalized citizens all over the world—and there are millions of us—she is this wonderful, wonderful example," says Greg Macabenta, a columnist for the *Manila Times* who lives in California.

The Filipino population in the United States, according to Census Bureau figures, hovers around 2.4 million, with almost half residing in California. The New Jersey/New York area, as well as Hawaii, have substantial Filipino populations, followed by the Chicago and Washington metropolitan areas.

"She's one of our own, she's doing very well, and we share in the pride," Macabenta says. "We want to tell our children, 'Hey look, don't believe that canard about the glass ceiling in the United States. You can be as good as the best of them in the world.'"

Executive Chef

The White House kitchen, located in the East Wing, is in a way the heart of the executive residence, with a style reflective of the administration it serves. Eleanor Roosevelt offered the king and queen of England hot dogs. Lyndon Johnson loved his barbecue (Texas style, naturally). The Carters favored southern food, grits and country ham. Nancy Reagan, a stickler for detail, had "tryout menus" of classic French cuisine for state dinners and had Polaroids taken of how the food should be presented. And though Hillary Clinton favored contemporary low-fat menus, Bill was famous for his not-too-rare Big Mac cravings.

In the 44 years since the title "executive chef" was introduced to the White House by Jacqueline Kennedy, only five people have held the post before Comerford: Rene Verdon, Henry Haller, Jon Hill, Pierre Chambrin and Scheib.

"Cris will surely bring her own flair to this job. But the pressure is different now that she's the boss," says Roland Mesnier, who was White House pastry chef for 25 years—he retired in July 2004—and worked with Comerford for nine years. He still remembers that Chilean sea bass she asked him to taste, and goes on and on about how the fish "was so very flaky and white and just extraordinary." "Hers is a job that is extremely demanding, and she'll have to be focused at all times, which I'm confident she'll be. In my experience with her, she doesn't do one day better than another day. The minute she steps in that kitchen, the second she's in there, Cris is focused."

She'll be paid somewhere between $80,000 and $100,000 annually, with no overtime, and will be in charge of five full-time employees, though that number can rise to 25 for large parties, state dinners and, of course, the White House Easter Egg Roll. She's an early riser, which helps—you never know just when President Bush, usually up at around 5:15 a.m., will want his breakfast.

So what will the White House kitchen run by Comerford look like, feel like, taste like?

Only Comerford knows.

The Comerfords returned from their vacation late Thursday night. The next morning, the new executive chef was back at work.

Apl.de.ap: Hip-Hop Musician

Apl.de.ap, as interviewed by Benjamin Pimentel

Allan Pineda, who uses the stage name Apl.de.ap, was born September 28, 1974, in Pampanga, Philippines. He is best known for his work in the Black Eyed Peas, a hip-hop band based in Los Angeles, California. At the age of fourteen, Apl was adopted and immigrated to the United States. His family in the Philippines was reluctant to see him go, but hoped his adopted family in the United States could provide a more comfortable life for him. After finishing high school, he joined his future Black Eyed Peas band mate will.i.am in a break-dancing group known as Tribal Nation.

In 2004 Apl's life story, including his sad parting from his family in the Philippines, was turned into a TV miniseries titled Maalaala Mo Kaya *(Will You Remember) for Philippine television. In this interview with Benjamin Pimentel, Apl discusses how his identity as a Filipino American artist informs the way he crafts his work. He cites Filipino music as influencing his songwriting, and expresses his pleasure with visits to the Philippines. Benjamin Pimentel is a staff writer for the* San Francisco Chronicle. *He is also the author of* Rebolusyon!: A Generation of Struggle in the Philippines.

In the most offbeat selection in "Monkey Business," Apl.de.ap of Black Eyed Peas raps on a song called "Bebot" about the joys of eating with one's fingers, drinking with friends and a popular Filipino delicacy called balut.

You have to be a particular kind of Peas fan to completely get it: "Bebot" is in Tagalog.

Apl.de.ap, as interviewed by Benjamin Pimentel, "No Matter How Successful He Gets, Black Eyed Peas' Apl Never Forgets His Roots in a Filipino Barrio, and His All Tagalog Hip-Hop Hit Proves It," *San Francisco Chronicle*, August 8, 2005, p. C1. Copyright 2005 The Chronicle Publishing Co. Reproduced with permission of The Chronicle Publishing Co., conveyed through Copyright Clearance Center, Inc.

Born and raised in the Philippines, Apl said he was encouraged to write the song after the incredible success Black Eyed Peas has enjoyed since their breakthrough album, "Elephunk." "Since we've made it in the business now, I'm able to go back home," he said in a phone interview. "I'm getting more practice in my Tagalog and Kapampangan," he added, referring to another Philippine language from his native province of Pampanga. "That inspired me to write more in Tagalog."

A Tagalog Chorus

It is not the first time that Black Eyed Peas ... has experimented with Tagalog. "The Apl Song" in "Elephunk" featured a Tagalog chorus from a Filipino folk band.

But in "Monkey Business," Apl included not just a chorus but an entire song in his native tongue. That underscores his attitude toward his ethnic identity. It's not just another footnote or curious factoid in Apl's career—he embraces it, flaunts it and would willingly get onstage to sing loudly—as he does in Bebot—"Filipino! Filipino! Filipino!"

Filipino Pride

"I'm proud of who I am, where I came from, what I was born into, and I would represent that till I die," he said. "As much as I could put in this music business, I want to involve who I am and my culture."

As an immigrant who hasn't completely lost his Filipino accent, he said he never got seriously bogged down by the FOB—"fresh off the boat" or "fresh off the Boeing"—label.

"I know a lot of Filipinos are concerned of (being called) FOB," he said. "I see that as FOBulous, because you have a different sense in you. Being from the Philippines, you have a different way of looking at life."

For that attitude and his music, Apl has become a legend in the Filipino American community and in the Philippines, where he grew up in a poor, working class family in Sapang Bato, a small barrio in Pampanga, north of Manila.

It was a tough life, but one that he celebrates in "The Apl Song."

"Listen closely yo, I got a story to tell

A version of my ghetto where life felt for real

Some would call it hell but to me it was heaven . . .

We makin' it happen, from nothin' to somethin'

That's how we be survivin' back in my homeland . . ."

Influence of Filipino Music

The song includes a Tagalog chorus from "Balita" ("News") by a well-known Filipino folk group called Asin (Salt) who, Apl said, was his favorite group in the Philippines.

Pendong Aban, one of Asin's members, said the group felt honored by Apl's acknowledgement of Asin's influence on his music. "We seldom hear how our songs impact our listeners' lives," he said in an e-mail.

Apl has even helped Asin cross the Philippines' stiff class hierarchy. Aban said the group had been popular among the poor and working class segments of Philippine society. But "The Apl Song" helped expose the group to a new generation of young listeners, including those from rich families who embraced American hip-hop culture.

"Balita" is a political song that talked about the repression and violence many Filipinos endured during the regime of the late dictator Ferdinand Marcos. The lyrics speak of a "land stained with blood" where "hearts are crying out."

Apl adapted the song to talk about his personal odyssey. "Now that I'm able to incorporate all types of music into hip-hop, I had the idea that that would be a dope idea because it explains where I came from," he said. "It's like I brought with me the 'news' on what happened to my own life."

Life in the Philippines

Apl's biological father was a U.S. serviceman who left him and his mother, Christina Pineda, before he was born. Apl, a.k.a. Allan Pineda, grew up with four brothers and two sisters supported by his mother.

Growing up in a former U.S. colony, he was exposed early to American pop music. He said his mother liked listening to Stevie Wonder, the Beatles and Eagles, as well as to Asin. "I would take the jeepney all the way to Angeles City, and that's how I got introduced to break dancing," he said. "I would see kids at the corner break-dancing and I'm like, 'I wanna do that.'"

At 14, he was adopted by a Southern California attorney. Apl still has vivid memories of his departure. "I left in the afternoon, and it was the saddest sunset ever. I didn't know where I was going. I was 14, and I'm getting on this plane by myself, and I could see the sun set."

Life in Los Angeles

Growing up in the Los Angeles area, he struggled with life as a teenage immigrant. "I would get chased from junior high school to my house every day," he recalled. "All these kids are like, 'Where you from?' And I was like, 'From Philippines.'"

He burst out laughing, then added: "After that, I was like, 'OK, that's not for me.'"

"You know, I could have easily joined the gangs that were surrounding me," he said. "I was exposed to that. But I chose dancing instead. That led me in a good direction."

A friendship with William Adams, a.k.a. will.i.am, evolved into a showbiz partnership as the duo, who took on the name Atban Klann, hit L.A.'s hip-hop/break-dance circuit.

Taboo, a.k.a. Jaime Gomez, later joined the team which then took on the name Black Eyed Peas. After two albums, the group brought in R&B singer Fergie, a.k.a. Stacy Ferguson, for "Elephunk." The album became a hit, and a selection, "Let's Get It Started," won the group their first Grammy.

Reflection

For Apl, success has given him more time to reflect on his roots and focus on the family he left behind. "Coming from the Philippines my whole goal was to support my family and have a better living situation," he said. "Trying to pursue my dream took up a lot of my time, and I got separated from my family a little bit . . . I was separated from my brothers and sisters. Some good things happened to them and some bad things happened to some of them."

The most stunning blow from the separation was his younger brother's suicide. "The Apl Song" is also a tribute to Arnel Pineda. A line in the tune goes:

Sometimes life's stresses get you down on your knees,

Oh brother how I wish I could have helped you out. . .

"That's what made me write that song," Apl said of his loss. "He was growing up and I was growing up, and I had to do what I had to do to make it in this world. I just wish he could have waited a little longer."

Returning Home

Whenever he goes back home, the first thing he does upon reaching Barrio Sapang Bato is to visit the local cemetery to light candles and bring flowers for his brother and his late grandparents.

Then, he said, he asks his mom to cook shrimp stew and chicken adobo. "I just go off on the food," he said. "She likes doing it. She wakes me up at 5 in the morning. It's like, 'Come on, we need to go to the palengke (market) and pick some stuff.' And I'm like, '5 in the morning?' But I guess that's when you get the fresh stuff."

He hopes to bring his mom and other family members to the United States. He has no plans yet for starting his own family, he said. "Gotta save first," he said. "I still gotta bring my whole family here. That's my goal right now."

He doesn't rule out the possibility of returning to his homeland to live. "I want to build resorts over there," he said, mentioning Boracay Island in central Philippines that reputedly has among the most beautiful beaches in the world.

Apl is also working on a solo collection of Tagalog rap geared to what has quickly turned into a solid fan base in his homeland. "The reception is unbelievable," he said of how Filipinos have reacted to him and his music.

Critical Reception

Eric Caruncho, a music critic based in Manila, said "The Apl Song" was a big hit in the Philippines and gave young Filipinos "someone to root for." Writer Jim Ayson said having a song with Tagalog lyrics in one of the biggest selling albums of the year was "mind boggling." "It's good he never forgot his roots," he said.

In "Bebot"—Filipino slang for "chick"—Apl is clearly having more fun in looking back at his Filipino roots.

Hey friends, listen to me,

Here's a true Filipino

From Barrio Sapang Bato,

Moved to L.A.

To help out my mom,

For it was a hard life we led

But I'm proud of my color

To eat, I use my fingers

Rice and chicken adobo

Balut sold on the street corner

Pass the glass, buddy

Let's have a drink!

"I experienced that type of lifestyle, and when I go back home, that's how it is still," he said. "I like buying balut from the vendor at the corner of the street."

That's perhaps the clearest proof of Apl's connection to his homeland.

Balut is boiled duck egg with a semi-developed embryo. Although it is a popular Philippine delicacy, it is unappetizing to many, particularly non-Filipinos. Apl spoke proudly of his "expertise" on how to eat it.

"You shake it up then you suck the juice first," he said. "Then you break down the egg and then you eat the soft part and then there's the hard part at the end and you've got to dip that with some salt. . . . I could do that with my eyes closed in the dark . . . But you gotta have a beer with that."

Chronology

1565

New Spain, under the rule of King Philip II, colonizes the Islas de Filipinas (The Philippine Islands). Spanish colonial rule lasts for more than three hundred years.

1587

Filipino "Luzon Indians" land in Morro Bay, California.

1763

Filipino sailors, known as "Manila men," desert Spanish trade ships and establish the fishing village of St. Malo in southern Louisiana.

1815

Manila men participate as soldiers in the War of 1812 in the Battle of New Orleans.

1848

A contingent of Filipinos settles in Mariposa County, California, and establishes the camp of Tulitos during the California Gold Rush.

1896

The Philippine Revolution of 1896 ends three centuries of Spanish colonial rule.

1898

On June 12 revolutionary leader Emilio Aguinaldo declares Philippine independence. The United States defeats Spain at the end of the Spanish American War and declares sovereignty over the Philippines. The Philippine-American War begins.

1902

The Philippine-American War officially ends. The United States declares sovereignty over the Philippines.

1903

The *pensionados*, students on government scholarship from the Philippines, arrive in the United States.

1904

The World's Fair in St. Louis exhibits a group of Filipinos as a side-show attraction.

1905

California legislation bans marriage between whites and "Mongolians."

1906

The first Filipino contract laborers, known as *sakadas*, arrive in Hawaii to work on sugar plantations.

1911

Labor leader Pablo Manalpit organizes Filipino laborers in Hawaii and forms the Filipino Higher Wages Association.

1920

Immigration of Filipino farm laborers increases. Filipino sugar plantation workers in Hawaii strike to protest wage discrimination.

1924

The Johnson-Reed Act, also known as the Immigration Act of 1924, bans Asian immigration. Filipino plantation workers in Hawaii strike to protest working conditions.

1930

Anti-Filipino race riots erupt in Watsonville, California. The number of Filipinos serving in the U.S. Navy reaches twenty-five thousand.

1933

Filipino American Virgil Duyungan becomes founding president of the Cannery Workers' and Farm Laborers' Union in Seattle, Washington.

1934

Passage of the Tydings-McDuffie Act limits the immigration of Filipinos to fifty per year. This act also sets a ten-year timetable for Philippine independence.

1935

The Filipino Repatriation Act of 1935 offers paid passage to those Filipinos who wish to return to live in the Philippines. Fewer than twenty-two hundred Filipinos participate in this program.

1941

Japanese forces bomb Pearl Harbor, Hawaii, and invade the Philippines. The United States enters World War II.

1941–1945

Filipinos, U.S. nationals, are actively recruited for service in the U.S. military.

1942

American forces in the Philippines surrender to the Japanese.

1945

Japan surrenders control of the Philippines to American forces. After passage of the War Brides Act, many Filipinas married to American servicemen immigrate to the United States.

1946

The Philippines gains independence from the United States on July 4. The Luce-Celler Act grants naturalization rights to Filipino Americans. The immigration quota of Filipinos is raised to one hundred per year. The Rescission Act of 1946 is passed by Congress, stripping Filipino American soldiers of veterans benefits. Carlos Bulosan publishes *America Is in the Heart.*

1965

The Immigration Act of 1965 is liberalized to increase immigration of Filipinos into the United States.

1974

Benjamin Menor becomes the first Filipino American state supreme court judge (Hawaii).

1975

Eduardo Malapit becomes the first Filipino American mayor (Kauai, Hawaii).

1981

Gene Viernes and Silme Domingo, Filipino American labor activists, are murdered in Seattle, Washington.

1990

A provision of the Immigration and Naturalization Act of 1990 allows Filipino World War II veterans the right to become U.S. citizens.

1994

Benjamin J. Cayetano becomes the first Filipino American governor (Hawaii).

1999

The murder of Filipino American Joseph Ileto by white supremacist Buford Furrow draws attention to anti-Asian hate crimes.

2003

The Citizenship Retention and Re-Acquisition Act of 2003 permits dual citizenship in both the United States and the Philippines.

2006

The Smithsonian Institution celebrates the Filipino American centennial of immigration to the United States with fourteen programs across the United States.

For Further Research

Books

Veltisezar Bautista, *The Filipino Americans from 1763 to the Present: Their History, Culture, and Traditions*. Aurora, IL: Bookhaus, 2002.

Carlos Bulosan, *America Is in the Heart*. New York: Harcourt, Brace, 1941.

Cecilia Manguerra Brainard, *Journey of 100 Years: Reflection on the Centennial of Philippine Independence*. Santa Monica, CA: Philippine American Writers & Artists, 1999.

———, ed., *Growing Up Filipino: Stories for Young Adults*. Santa Monica, CA: Philippine American Writers & Artists, 2003.

H.W. Brands, *Bound to Empire: The United States and the Philippines*. New York: Oxford University Press, 1992.

Sucheng Chan, *Asian Americans, an Interpretive History*. Boston: Twayne, 1991.

Lorraine Jacobs Crouchett, *Filipinos in California: From the Days of the Galleons to the Present*. El Cerrito, CA: Downey Place, 1982.

Marina E. Espina, *Filipinos in Louisiana*. New Orleans: A.F. Laborde and Sons, 1988.

Yen Le Espiritu, *Home Bound: Filipino American Lives Across Cultures, Communities, and Countries*. Los Angeles: University of California Press, 2003.

Luis H. Francia and Eric Gamalinda, *Flippin': Filipinos on America*. New York: Rutgers University Press, 1996.

Dorothy B. Fujita-Rony, *American Workers, Colonial Power: Philippine Seattle and the Transpacific West, 1919–1941*, Berkeley: University of California Press, 2003.

Emil Guillermo, *AMOK: Essays from an Asian American Perspective.* San Francisco: Asian Week, 1999.

Jessica Hagedorn, *Dogeaters.* New York: HarperCollins, 1990.

Emily Noelle Ignacio, *Building Diaspora: Filipino Community Formation on the Internet.* New Brunswick, NJ: Rutgers University Press, 2005.

Stanley Karnow, *In Our Image: America's Empire in the Philippines.* New York: Ballantine, 1990.

Jonathon Y. Okamura, *Imagining the Filipino American Diaspora: Transnational Relations, Identities, and Communities.* New York: Garland, 1998.

Barbara M. Posadas, *The Filipino Americans.* Westport, CT: Greenwood, 1999.

Norman Reyes, *Child of Two Worlds: An Autobiography of a Filipino American or Vice Versa.* Colorado Springs, CO: Three Continents, 1995.

Maria P.P. Root, ed., *Filipino Americans: Transformation and Identity.* Thousand Oaks, CA: Sage, 1997.

E. San Juan Jr., *From Exile to Diaspora: Versions of the Filipino Experience in the United States.* Boulder, CO: Westview, 1998.

Craig Scharlin and Lilia V. Villanueva, *Philip Vera Cruz: A Personal History of Filipino Immigrants and the Farmworkers Movement.* Seattle: University of Washington Press, 2000.

Daniel B. Schirmer and Stephen R. Shalom, eds., *The Philippines Reader: A History of Colonialism, Neocolonialism, Dictatorship and Resistance.* Boston: South End, 1987.

Reuben S. Seguritan, *We Didn't Pass Through the Golden Door: The Filipino American Experience.* USA: Institute for Filipino American Research, 1997.

Ronald Takaki, *In the Heart of Filipino America: Immigrants from the Pacific Isles.* New York: Chelsea House, 1995.

Web Sites

Americans of Filipino Descent (www.personal.Anderson.ucla. edu/eloisa.borah/filfaqs.htm). A collection of information about Filipino American history and culture compiled by research librarian Eloisa Gomez Borah, member of the Filipino American Librarians Association.

Filipino American National Historical Society (www.fanhs-national.org). The mission statement of this Seattle, Washington, based organization is "to promote understanding, education, enlightenment, appreciation and enrichment through the identification, gathering, preservation, and dissemination of the history and culture of Filipino Americans in the United States."

Filipino American Resources (www.seattleu.edu/lemlib/web _archives/Filipino/history). Compiled by the Lemieux Library at Seattle University, this Web site features links to Filipino American arts, culture, sports, history, issues, literature, newspapers, and magazines.

Filipino Americans.Net (filipinoamericans.net). Bookhaus Publishers' Web project provides a collection of information on the history and culture of Filipinos in the United States, as well as links to news and recipes.

The Philippine History Site (opmanong.ssc.Hawaii.edu/PAW Links.html). This Web site, created by the Office of Multicultural Student Services at the University of Hawaii (Operation Manong) and The Filipino-American Historical Society of Hawaii, focuses on: the Philippine Revolution, the Philippine-American War, and Filipino migration to the United States.

Index